The
ETCH
Anthology
2015

Vocamus Press, Guelph, Ontario

ISBN 13: 978-1-928171-17-1 (pbk)
ISBN 13: 978-1-928171-18-8 (ebk)

Vocamus Press
130 Dublin Street, North
Guelph, Ontario, Canada
N1H 4N4

www.vocamus.net

2015

CONTENTS

GRADES 11 - 12

Preface

The stories in this collection are the winners and runners up from the Guelph Public Library's 2015 Teen Writing Contest. They were judged and arranged in the collection by grade level.

The cover of the collection was made using the winning entry of the Guelph Public Library's 2014 Cover Contest, created by Shehryar Saharan, a Grade 12 student at Centennial Collegiate Vocational Institute. The promotional material for the launch was made using the second place image, created by Nik MacMillan, a Grade 12 student from Guelph Collegiate Vocational Institute.

Writerly mentorship was provided by Guelph area authors – Lisa Browning, James Clarke, Douglas Davey, Alexander Dundas, Heather Embree, Laurie Gardiner, Bill Hulet, Clifford Jackman, John Jantunen, Michelle Jay, Burl Levine,

CONTENTS

Laura Lush, Sean McCabe, Don Moore, Shane Neilson, and Nicholas Ruddock.

The stories were judged by Elissa Davidson, Jeremy Luke Hill, John Jantunen, and Ben Robinson. The contest was organized and arranged by Elissa Davidson of the Guelph Public Library. The book's cover and interior were designed by Jeremy Luke Hill of Vocamus Press.

GRADES 11 - 12

Footsteps in the Snow

Catherine Meng

*Inspired by the piano prelude
"Des Pas Sur La Neige" by Debussy.*

The soft crunch of snow.

Chilled air–

And stillness.

Footsteps in an empty field of knee-deep powder, whiter and as pure as the soul of a newborn baby. Above are glum and clouded skies, wrapping the land with an engulfing, cold embrace. The soft fall of snow had passed and was no more, taking with it the serenity and peace of the atmosphere and leaving only the tension-filled frigid air. In the distance, a gray, desolate church lay ahead, bare and exposed to the harsh beauty of nature. And there is a man – a speck on a blank canvas – leaving a trail of footsteps behind him, as he slowly makes his way across the clearing.

Numbness. Every step more difficult than the last, and each foot forward requiring increased effort. Every thought of her making every moment harder and harder to bear.

But his heart was heavy, frozen and unable to feel. The sadness chilled him, until emotion could no longer enter his soul. He was so fragile, that it pained him to even move at the speed at which he was walking. He felt as if his body would burst into a million shards if he dared to quicken his pace. So he proceeded forward, and as he plodded, his feet slowly sunk deep into the cotton snow one after the other.

The thought of her haunted him, echoing in his mind; the memories of them together slowly leaked away. But he held on before they completely escaped the grasp of his mind, before they could slip away like sand.

Remembering her smile casted sunrays unto him, thawing his heart of ice little by little, reminding him of what he had to keep alive.

But why hold on? Everything that was his had been taken away from him, frozen, then shattered with a hammer. He had tried to pick it all up and put it back together, piece by piece, but how could he when the largest fragment was gone and had melted away?

A quiet emotion approached and crept into the back of his mind. A mournful sigh, full with melancholy inched its way through his body. It grew, his heart slowly beginning to unfreeze and he was finally able to feel the great sorrow within it.

All the while, he kept on walking, treading painstakingly as the impact of her death hit him in the most tender spot in his spirit. Drowning in heartache, every cell within his body welled up with agony – and stillness. Engulfed with misery, his emotions became more clear, and he could hear nothing but the delicate chime of bells echoed from the church. The pure sound resonated and floated in the atmosphere, suspended by the frozen air around him. And like his grief, they slowly drifted and settled on the surface of the snow.

He stopped. And remained still.

He was afraid that if he moved any further, he would disturb the emotions that had come to rest peacefully on top of the snow in which he had been walking. Motionless, he allowed the ice to freeze his heart once more, crystallizing his soul and trapping his spirit in eternal winter.

Suddenly, there was light. A sparkle of sun, peering through the gray, a lining of silver threaded through the hem of the surrounding clouds. A single ray that thaws a heart of ice. And for the last time, he embraced it's warmth instead of denying it. He let himself become engulfed with pure agony and grief; he let his heart cry, he let his heart bleed.

Footsteps in the Snow

The pulse of a heart, free of grief.
A weeping heart.
Bleeding, with every droplet falling in the snow, blossoming and tainting the innocent white with the crimson in his veins. Red jewels of sorrow, ruby tokens of his everlasting grief.

And a thawed heart,

that slowly pulses

into

nothing

leaving only

footsteps

in the snow.

Volvox

Jodre Datu

This is my *execution*.

We are in the bathroom, and by now I am used to its images, its associated mental dread, scrubbing every day the imprints of dirty feet and dirty business. I do it happily, this scrubbing and dusting and wiping and sponging, because happiness is all that I'm supposed to be given. Other feelings are myths, like fairy tales that Mother tells Child at night time.

The tub of water, hot water, is filled right to the edges so that little clear drops leak out. Beside the tub, the family stands in a triangle and I am in the centre of Mother, Father, at the base, and Child, at the top vertex. They tell me to stand still, and I follow, become a tree rooted into the porcelain tile. I smile, because they want me to. Because it is programmed within me that it is polite to smile. Like commandments engraved in stone.

Mother holds a sheet of paper. She says, "Are we doing this right?" She scans the page with dull gray eyes.

Father takes the paper from her snowy hands. "Yes, I think so."

"Did you add salt to the water?" Mother says. Tilts her head. Humanly.

"What does salt do?" replies Father. He looks at me. "Ask it."

"Volvox," Mother says. My head flings toward her. That word is my name, a trumpet calling.

"How may I serve you?" I say.

"Are we doing this right?"

I search, electricity fires, and I answer: *"In order to dispose of a Volvox model, approximately 110L of water is required. Simply fill a tub full of water and instruct your model to step inside and lay on his back. Immediately the skin should deteriorate as well as the metal skeleton inside. Within an hour the model will be gone completely. Adding salt accelerates the process."*

I breathe, sensing something well in my stomach, an earthquake. It feels like fear, and that word, floating in thought, is strange: feel. I shouldn't know what that is.

"Alright," Father says. "I'll get the salt."

"In the kitchen. Top cupboard. Just grab the whole bag."

"I will."

Father walks out. I watch Mother break the triangle also, march to the sink and splash water onto her face. Child watches her, not understanding why any of them are here, but happy anyways. Child carries a doll in her hands, which has stringy red hair and small eyes and bright lips. Made of cotton. Lines of crayon all over the hem of the doll's dress, as if Child was unsatisfied with the original. I am like this doll, coloured and fixed to be something I'm not, smiling with bright, plastic lips, permanently oriented.

Mother comes back to the triangle. "Mom," Child says. Her voice is a soft puddle, a pool of clean rain. She tugs at Mother's white dress. "What are we doing to Volvox?"

My head turns, snaps sharply at her last word. Mother's hand touches Child's small back.

"We are making him sleep," Mother says.

"Why?" Child says. Sadness leaks from her voice.

"He's done," Mother says. She's lying; they're done with me. "We've used him all up."

"Oh. Who's going to clean my room, now?"

"The new one. We're buying a new one."

That word also. I do not like it, because underneath it means to replace.

Child says, "Will the new one make macaroni and cheese?"

"Yes."

"Will the new one carry me on his back?'

"Yes, dear. Further than before."

"Will the new one still be my brother?"

9

It is a sad question. For some reason, sadness hovers above me, I don't have to search. I can just feel it. Like the shadow of a cloud.

Mother cups Child's red cheeks. "Of course, dear. You need a strong brother who can protect you."

"But I can protect myself, I think," she says.

"You'll like the new one even more," Mother says, ignoring her. "It will move more quickly, be more powerful. It will last longer. It will be better."

* * * * *

Before this, I am the incarnation of the word "new". This word makes me pristine, wraps around me, glows like a moon in the ocean. I wait.

I'm in my packaging, my mind rests, only a whisper of electricity swaying in my head. Not enough to be "off", but not enough to be "on" either. In between these two words, like a toddler without memories, just a simple sheet of a body and nothing more. But still capable of seeing. Of listening.

The house is quiet. Sleek furniture tosses the light. The couches and chairs are made of black leather, cubic and ordinary. Flowers inserted in odd places, off-centered on the coffee table, behind a family photo, jutting beneath the picture frames. The chandelier scatters light like soft, gold snow. A rich house, a boring home.

It is Child who takes me out of the chrome silver packaging, excitedly, unwraps the black wire flossed around my wrists, unwinds the cotton swathed over my flesh. I come with tan skin, peachy, a request from Mother and Father, and a simple white shirt and white pants. Buttoned. Tight.

"He's beautiful," Child says. She holds my arm, feels the hard metal within, knocks on it hesitantly, as if asking to enter a friend's home, and looks to Father.

Mother and Father both have their noses scrunched, their nostrils flared.

"I don't know," Father says to Mother. "He has small arms. Are you sure we ordered the right one?"

Mother squints her eyes. "Of course I'm sure," Mother says.

He grabs my shoulders and turns me around. He runs his hand down my back, breathes in sharply. "I don't know. I thought he would look better. More built."

"I don't care how he..." Child says. Ignored.

"Well, we can try it out," Mother says. "And return it if we need to."

Father finds the groove in the back of my neck, just below the base of my skull, just above the bar code. He puts his thumb there and his fingerprint matches an internal prophecy. He ignites me.

A flash of light, and the illusion of life presses into me: first my chest, then my stomach, then all over. The electricity sparks many processes all at once, an ecstasy, rapture, a rush of positive and negative charges tangled in bundles.

11

Volvox

Flowing and flowing and flowing. Inside my head is like soup.

My first words are supposed to be: "How may I serve you?" It's an automatic call, a ritual, placed deep in the programming. It's a sign that we work, that we are built to serve.

Instead, I look at Mother and Father, then at my hands, then at my arms. It is this moment that makes me suspect I am different from the other Volvox models. Because I feel uncomfortable in my own body, because I don't want to serve. Because I can suspect I am different, because I am different. There must have been an error in my creation, I'm sure of it, a little tampering in the factory, circuitry imbalanced, chemicals spilled. Enough to create thought. But they hate this. They hate work, they hate thought. They like their rich house, they like being bored, being boring.

"I would like to serve you," I say. My first words are lies. "He's beautiful," Child says, still holding my arms. No one listens.

* * * * *

Father returns from his trip, enters the bathroom with sharp movement of his arms, swaying and swaying, with determination. He carries a brown bag – Liberty Natural Sea Salt, Rich In Minerals, printed in blue. He looks at Mother, his wife, old love whisked in their gazes, and pours the salt into the bath tub. The white swirls inside, mixing and disappearing, colliding and becoming invisible. He sighs, like it is hard work. Like he knows what work is.

Mother looks at me. Child looks away. "Go on, Volvox," Mother says, waves her hand. "Step inside the bathtub, now."

Mother's command drenches me with purpose, makes the codes and the processes weep with joy. It moves my muscles, one joint of metal at a time, flexing, flexing. I watch my legs shift their weight, carry the energy forward and backward, resonate. I watch my legs take me out of the centre of the triangle, my plastic eyes turning and jumping. My leg rises and almost reaches the water, the edge of it shimmering, twinkling in light. I see my reflection – glossy, shiny. Fake.

I stop.

I turn toward Mother, grab her arm.

"No," I say.

She steps backward, pulls away, as if I've spoken murder. Father, too, rushes toward Mother to comfort her. Tears melt the white of her eyes into red. Her hand rushes to her arm, worriedly, as if touched by a phantom.

"You're scaring us," Father snaps. His face matches the colour of Mother's red lipstick. "Step into the water and turn off."

Mother's eyebrows draw inward; earthquakes are inside of her.

"No," I say again. I like this word.

Saturday Morning Drive

Kiara Julien

Justin was out on his Saturday morning drive before most people had even gotten up. It had become something of a habit. With windows rolled down, wind blowing swiftly through his close-cut brown hair, he sped along the highways with no particular destination in mind. He usually skipped going to the movies or a club Friday nights so he could drive Saturday morning.

It all started when he had learned how to drive. Justin's dad had kept an old pick-up truck to give to him when he was old enough, its previous owner leaving it behind for him.

Justin always drove with the windows down and regretted the days that were too cool or too wet to do so. He became obsessed with the air rushing into his lungs, breathing it in with deep breaths that lowered his heart beat. He could never get enough, as if there were little bits of smoke in his chest that would never disappear.

He was a practiced thinker, taking the time to search through his mind, momentarily reliving his memories. He always got stuck on one, the whole memory broken into miniscule fragments preventing him from truly recollecting. Like a strip of film with entire sections cut out, he saw the scene play before his eyes: he was focused on his comic book collection beneath his bed that was burning away. Through a wall of smoke, he saw a shadowy silhouette appear on the other side of his bed. Before the silhouette reached him, his eyes forced themselves shut. He felt himself being lifted off the ground by a strong grip. When he could open his eyes again, he was no longer in his bedroom, but outside, and his short breaths sucked in the cool air around him. The film stopped short and the scene dissolved, leaving him.

Justin focused on his truck rolling forward on the roads. Some roads were smooth, the pavement flowing into the car up from the wheels, through him, then down the rear tires. Others were bumpy, snagging at his insecurities with every unexpected jolt. There couldn't be one without the other and Justin embraced the combination fully.

They took him left and right, travelling in every direction through his hometown. On his right was the park his father took him to after dinner nearly every day for the majority of his childhood. Quickly the lush park was behind him and the quiet road took him to the only hospital in town. He had only been a patient once as a young boy, after the night he couldn't remember.

When Justin awoke in the hospital, he was with his father and a doctor. They were telling him his mother was dead. "Mum didn't make it," he had been told, her injuries too severe, a result of her doing everything to save her son's life. He hated euphemisms. He hated them almost as much as being unable to remember his mother giving her life to save him.

A soft, cautionary sound stirred him from his thoughts. He needed to get gas and adjusted his route to the closest gas station.

When he arrived at the gas station, there was only one other person there. He thought it curious that the car the other person was driving was the exact same as his. The polished midnight blue paint, the shiny silver rims, even the dent on the left side of the back bumper. He thought he must be imagining the similarities, but they were undeniable.

He quickly filled up and went into the little shop to pay. Inside, he stood in line behind the driver of the other car – a young woman. When she turned around and Justin saw her face, he got a feeling that he had seen her before, that he'd known her for a long time. He felt the pain only caused by nostalgia flicker through his chest, all the way to his extremities. He looked at her in shock.

The young woman noticed him looking at her and her

eyes brightened, a radiant smile taking shape on her lips, a soft "hello" rolling off her tongue.

He wondered why she smiled at him and could not remember who she could be. He could see her lips move but didn't hear any sound escape from them.

Her eyes began to lose their light as she realized that he could not remember her. She did not let her smile waver, but looked away from his face before walking out and driving away.

Justin noticed the clerk staring at him and quickly finished his business at the gas station before continuing his drive.

Fresh air filling his lungs again, he tried to figure out where he might have seen that woman before. He was frustrated that his memory was failing him again, but he scanned through each piece of the puzzle anyway. By the time he arrived at the park where he would stop, he still hadn't figured it out.

Justin pulled up on the side of the road and got out of his car. He walked into the park when from the corner of his eye he caught a glimpse of the identical car that had been at the gas station. He began to feel worried, but continued walking anyway. He approached a bench that he liked to imagine had taken the shape of his behind and took a seat. He was completely alone, other than the small ducks swimming effortlessly across the pond in front of him. Behind him trees rustled, but Justin didn't move from his spot on the bench. The woman appeared, walking gracefully, almost heavenly towards him.

She gently placed her hand on his shoulder.

He didn't react. He was thinking about the woman, but he couldn't remember. From his wallet, he pulled out the only picture he had of his mother: she was looking down at him as a baby, cradled in her arms. Her face escaped him, too, as it always did since the night of the fire.

She stayed standing behind him for a while, looking at the picture with him.

He replaced the photo and stood up to leave.

She watched him climb into her old car before fading away, ready for the next Saturday morning drive when he would think of her again.

Advancements

Emma Chiera

This is a story about a trip.

It doesn't have much of a plot – or a point – but it's a nice little story, I think. It takes place in one of my favourite cities. A beautiful city, made even more beautiful by the fact that at the time of my story, I had never been there before. I think everything is more striking the first time.

I graduated from high school a few years ago, near the top of my class. After that, I went straight to McGill University. I wasn't a brilliant girl, but I had a keen sense of curiosity and awareness. I was certain that university was where I would learn about the world and gather new experiences. It was all I really wanted.

But after my first year, I was dissatisfied. I found myself longing for an education about society, people, and relationships; so, I took a year off school to travel. I spoke several European languages and longed to explore that continent. But my pockets had not the depth of my verbal skills; thus I settled on a big city, Chicago, as my destination. I soon wound up in the midst of America.

During my first days in the windy city, I was astounded by a lot of things: the desirable warmth in late April; the mass amounts of people; and the air of hope, danger and opportunities that surrounded the city like a fog. But what stunned me most was Chicago itself.

I brought a bike with me and spent many hours exploring the majestic city in awe. Chicago, though in Illinois, sits right on Lake Michigan; a big, blue, beautiful body of water. There are also two turquoise rivers running through the city, interlocking near State Street. Chicago's subway loop and grid-like avenues run across bridges, framed by towering modern skyscrapers and contrasting ancient buildings rich with history. The intricately detailed architecture was what amazed me most, I think. Or perhaps it was the overwhelming masses of successful people swarming around glamourous shopping malls. Or maybe it was the gorgeous waterfront beaches, harbours and ports, all bathed by the sun and salt. All of this I gaped at as I rode past couples flagging down cabs, buskers swallowing flames, and men in suits checking their expensive watches.

For a while, I didn't know what I was doing in this strange and wonderful place, and I didn't care either. I settled into a dirty little apartment at the edge of town, and for the first few weeks, I was in a blissful paradise. I went to baseball games, visited the beach, shopped, sat in cafés and comedy clubs, and checked out every corny tourist attraction. I wanted to soak up the city I was so enamoured with.

Eventually I realized that money was quickly draining from my wallet and I had no means of replenishing it. So I got a job at Lindsey's Café and Eatery, waiting tables from 8 AM to 2 PM every day. It allowed me lots of free time to explore the city further. I never grew tired of strolling down the busy streets and taking pictures of the water. It was the height of my life.

In early July, I was growing eager for company. I remembered that a couple of friends in high school had gone to the University of Michigan, so I made some calls and set up a lunch date. Over the phone, they seemed eager to reconnect. I was already imagining the possibilities; having friends nearby could make my Chicago adventure that much better.

So, one day after work, I met up with Jessica and Emily for deep-dish pizza and catching-up. As I pushed through the revolving door, the girls squealed.

"We're so happy to see you!" Jessica cried, smothering me in a hug. "It's been way too long!"

Happiness engulfed me as we chatted, standing in line to order. I hadn't realized how much I'd longed for companionship until that moment. Our conversation flowed lightly and freely as we took our pizza and headed to the nearest wooden table.

Advancements

As we sat down, Emily's phone dinged. She took it out of her pocket and began to type, her nimble fingers twitching systematically across the tiny keyboard. She answered the message, but to my surprise, didn't put the phone away. Then Jessica pulled out her cell phone, too, and checked it. She murmured to Emily, "There's free WiFi here."

Emily nodded and took a sloppy bite of her pizza, never taking her eyes off her little device.

So I sat across from these two instant zombies, their faces illuminated by a strange luminescent shade of green from the glow of the screens. And I sat. And sat. And I kept trying to make conversation, and failed. I had a phone in my bag too, but I felt no desire to take it out. It was a tool, not entertainment. So the awkwardness grew.

I finished my pizza. Then I went to the bathroom. Then I sat. And I took a drink of water. And I sat some more. I crossed my legs. Then my arms. I uncrossed them. I examined my nails. I sat.

Eventually I announced, "I'm going to take off, I have something to do."

At first there was no reaction. Then, as I stood up, Jessica looked up from her phone and said, "Oh, no!"

"Stay," said Emily.

I shook my head, promised to call them, and grabbed my bag.

As I made my way to the door, I looked around, and for a moment panic rose in my throat nightmarishly. All I saw was people looking down at phones, tablets and laptops, having no human interaction whatsoever. I pushed my way outside and breathed in gulps of fresh air.

A few weeks later, I met a man. I was on a bench in Millennium Park, sketching the scenery. The man stopped to ask me for directions. I gave them, and he asked what I was doing. I showed him my work, and he laughed and said that it was terrible. I laughed too, admitting he was right. (I don't have much artistic talent.)

The man and I began seeing each other. His named was David Brussels, and he was a corporate worker; therefore obsessed with technology. He embraced every new version of whatever device Apple or Google presented to the world. I had no interest in any of this, but was forced to put up with non-stop text messages from him all the time. But I put up with noticeably larger cell phone bills because I greatly enjoyed his company. He took me anywhere I wanted in Chicago: we went to every fancy restaurant and classy event we could find. Now, looking back, I wonder who I was really in love with: him or the city.

David did all his important work via email, so he carried around a little tablet everywhere he went. He found my aversion to it quite amusing, and laughed at my look of disgust every time he pulled it out of his bag.

"Technology is the future of our generation," he always said. "Don't get left behind."

David was the one to show me the world that I had so blissfully ignored. Chicago was a very different society than what I was used to, and I had failed to see it before. Slowly,

Advancements

I began to notice industrialization everywhere. At the park, young girls were messaging their friends. In coffee shops, men and women were absorbed by laptops. Bookstores became Apple stores. My CD player broke and I got strange looks when I tried to buy a replacement. Times were changing, and I was lost.

I stopped seeing David. I blamed him entirely for ruining my beloved city. I could never see Chicago the same way again. Of course, I now realize that he didn't deserve my harsh treatment; he'd simply taught me to look around.

A month later, I left Chicago and headed back home. I couldn't bear to live there anymore. But I wasn't ready for what greeted me back home, either.

It was the same. Everything was the same. All I could see was electronic doom, and it broke my heart. Like David had said, I couldn't run from it. So I accepted it.

In 1871, an enormous fire wiped out the entire city of Chicago. Today, 1871 is the name of a Chicago-based technology incubator. It's a nod to the time when the city was forced to start over, using the resources at hand: something I had failed to do, unlike the rest of my generation.

I have a tablet now, and an iPhone, and an iPod, and a massive computer. My desktop background is a picture of Chicago – the ruins of it, after the great fire. I sometimes Skype my old friends from Michigan. I even found David on Facebook. I'm not getting left behind.

A Tradition of Books

Annie Zhang

Elizabeth curled further into the shadow of the bookshelf, hoping that she would not be noticed.

It worked, usually. A lot of people don't give enough credit to the remarkable concealing powers of a bookshelf. Sit beside one, stick your face among a decent amount of pages, and no one's the wiser.

Unfortunately, the person looking for her didn't fit into the general population when it comes to her tricks.

"There you are."

There was her mother, looking decidedly more annoyed than she had been two hours ago. She had definitely bottled up her fair dose of lecture. Her raven hair had escaped from its usual neat bun, leaving curly little strands all over the place, and her glasses were just a touch skewed. Anyone else would have appeared slightly ridiculous. It just made her mother look more stern.

"I wasn't hiding."

"Could have fooled me."

Elizabeth batted her eyelashes, giving her mother her famous doe eyes that would've coaxed at least a smile out of her father.

Alas, once again her mother proved herself not part of the general population susceptible to her charms.

"You're in the corner of the last listings of adult nonfiction. Not exactly where I expect someone who wishes to be found would be sitting."

"Plenty of people sit here."

Her mother rolled her eyes and stared at her, daring Elizabeth to self-examine her stained jeans, bird's nest of hair, and "the cake was a lie" t-shirt. "Lizzie, you could at least have told me you were coming here."

"It's the library. And me. It's not a great scientific equation to assess the likelihood of both of us occurring in the same circumstance."

"You hardly just 'occurred' here, Lizzie. You've been here for at least an hour too long."

"Well –"

There it was, the hand held up, demanding her to be silent. Lizzie had been waiting for that.

Even Elizabeth Beren knew there was a point to how much she could push her mother.

Leslie Beren flopped onto the nearest beanbag chair, yanked off her skewed glasses with obviously more force than necessary. There was something disturbing about the sight of her mother sitting on a beanbag chair, hair messy, noticeably tired.

The image of her mother had always consisted of a well-dressed, sophisticated woman sitting in a straight-backed chair, elegantly pushing up her glasses while flipping the pages of a worn paperback, all backlit by warm sunlight. Elizabeth always thought there should be a sign written above the image: "See kids? This is what you should aspire to read like when you grow up!"

"Lizzie, I know you've been angry with me recently…"

"Angry is too strong a word."

"Displeased –"

"I never said anything."

"You don't need to say anything. Your face could curdle milk these past weeks."

"Thanks, mom."

"Not your actual face, sweetie, you know what I mean. For God's sake, will you let me finish a sentence?"

Elizabeth made a small shrugging motion she hoped looked apologetic.

"I know you haven't been able to come to the library lately, and I certainly haven't been a scintillating conversationalist around the house," her mother began.

"No duh, you don't even read anymore."

This was probably one of those many moments when her mother considered strangling her daughter.

"No, Elizabeth. Because as you undoubtedly have noticed, we've been very busy."

That was the unavoidable point in the conversation, up front, with no sugar or frosting. Elizabeth bit her lip and played with the loose end of her jean hem, anything to keep herself from having to look at her mother in the eye.

"I know you don't like having someone new in the family. Much less a baby."

No, she didn't. But not quite for the reasons that her mother assumed.

"And I know you don't like the Nanny either."

"Lisa's fine," Elizabeth replied. "It's not about her."

"Well, you don't like being woken up four o'clock in the morning, but neither do I, Lizzie. Guess what? You don't actually have to deal with it, but I do. Maybe you're angry that you haven't been able to go the places you want, that we haven't accompanied you, or I haven't been reading or discussing books with you. That's what happens, Lizzie. Lisa is there for a reason, and we're not going to get rid of your brother, not even if it's for Christmas."

Looking at her mother's tired smile, she shook her head. "That was a lousy joke."

Her mother was right to a degree. No, she didn't like been woken up four o'clock in the morning by her brother's crying, so loud and piercing it felt like the sound nearly shattered the walls. She didn't like the nanny in the house, and it wasn't any repulsion towards Lisa herself, who was a perfectly courteous and nice person. She disliked the way things had been lately, yet not for the reasons her mother assumed.

"Yes, I don't like the fact you don't go the library any more or the fact you don't read or discuss books with me anymore. Yes, I don't like getting woken up four o'clock in the morning or how the house always smells like soiled diapers and sour milk –"

Her mom put her hand in her hands. "Elizabeth –"

"Just – let me finish a sentence, mom."

They both took a deep breath, breathing in the smell of paper and wood and ink, all smells they were familiar with. They both had spent more time in the library than they could count and could recognize its scent better than the back of their hands.

"I don't like it," Elizabeth continued. "But that doesn't mean I'm angry. If I'm angry, it's not at you or Lisa or Dad... much less David." She faltered at her brother's name. "It's because you're not letting me help."

Finally, she lifted the books up, letting her mother see what she had been reading.

"He's my little brother. I want to try," Elizabeth said. "I could help with taking care of him so you and Dad aren't so tired all the time. That's why I've been angry."

Her mother flipped through the two books, one a book on infant care, and one an illustrated storybook Elizabeth had loved as a little kid.

31

"So…yeah, that's why I was here so long," Elizabeth muttered. "And as for how angry I've been…it's just that you could've given me the chance to help as well. Maybe I'm not a nanny, but there are things I could learn about taking care of a baby."

There was a long pause before her mother spoke again: "Let's try bringing him to the library, shall we?"

A Day at the Park

Megan White

"No no no!"

Silvia moaned behind clenched teeth. She tore the paper of scattered prose from her notebook and scrunched it into a ball, throwing it onto the ground behind her.

She slumped over to lean on her elbows, yanking at her hair. This used to be so easy. She remembered the days when poetry was as mindless as breathing – when words would flow from her pen without her even thinking about it. She remembered the days when life was a dream, every aspect of it forming a perfectly plotted story from which she could derive her art.

She sighed and leaned back, crossing her arms. That was a long time ago.

A Day at the Park

She gazed at the seemingly fabricated scene around her. She sat on a cold black bench on the rim of an abandoned playground. The swings and slides were now rusted blades, the soccer field which surrounded it was as grey and sad as the sky above it. Silvia sighed. She remembered coming here as an enchanted little girl to write story after story after story, ideas flowing endlessly from her mind like a waterfall.

Now it seemed the only inspiration she could get was from everyone else's ideas. Her mind was blank. She lived no longer in a world of inspiration and wonder, but one of deprivation and routine – a world where people like Silvia didn't seem to belong.

She tried to escape her despair, but the voice of her father echoed in her head, "I will not tolerate a freak for a daughter! Did I raise you to throw away your life like this? Wasting your days away in a world that doesn't even exist? Wake up! The real world isn't in your books."

Silvia had run out of the house that morning and escaped to the park before he had the chance to finish. She couldn't handle another day like that. What was the point anymore?

Silvia closed her eyes.

Suddenly, a piercing screech tore through her thoughts. Silvia cringed, covering her ears. She looked around the park for the source of the sound, and caught sight of a little girl rocking gently back and forth on the swing set. She seemed completely oblivious to the deafening sound coming from the cables above her head. She sat in silence, staring down at her lap.

Silvia rolled her eyes – she had never been very fond of kids. She gritted her teeth and pushed on her knees to stand up. Normally she'd ignore this, but she couldn't put up with even minor annoyances right now.

She walked briskly across the park, kicking dust up at her feet. She reached out to grab the girl by the shoulder, when she heard the tiniest muffled hiccoughs. The girl was leaning over her lap with her hands on her face, letting tears gently fill her palms.

Silvia stood to the side of the little girl, staring at her awkwardly. For the first time in years her determination faltered. The girl was so scrawny, so frail – she looked almost like how Silvia felt.

"Hey, uh, kid," Silvia mumbled. "You know, uh, you're making a lot of noise."

The little girl kept crying into her hands and took no notice of her.

"Um, do you want to tell me what's wrong?"

The little girl cried a little harder.

"Look kid, would you stop crying so much?"

The girl glanced slowly up at Silvia through glossed eyes, her face gone blotchy red. She sniffled obnoxiously. "It's the park," she mumbled between sobs.

Silvia couldn't help a smile. "Yeah, I know it's not much, but you really don't have to cry over it."

"They're going to tear it down."

Silvia paused, taken aback. She felt her heart sink a little in her chest. She had few fond memories of her childhood, most of which resided here. She looked down at the ground. The girl continued sniffling into her hands, realizing Silvia wasn't going to help.

Silvia sighed and looked at her. "You like this park, huh?"

The girl sniffed. "Uh huh – daddy and I come here all the time to play. I like to play on the swings."

Silvia looked down at her feet, reminded of her father.

"I don't want the swings to go away."

Silvia couldn't help but laugh to herself. She smiled and stood upright. "Yeah, things are tough all over kid."

The little girl stared at the ground, thinking solemnly. Her voice perked up slightly. "My Daddy is an artist. He likes to draw pictures at the park."

Silvia stared into space. She wished she could remember caring about little things so much.

The girl curiously looked up at her. "Why do you come to the park?"

Silvia's face dropped – she was taken aback. Why would she care? Confused, she furrowed her eyebrow and looked at the girl. "Um, I," Silvia smiled, "I'm a writer. I come here to write."

The little girl's eyes widened and she stared up at Silvia in awe. "Really? You make stories?"

Silvia laughed and nodded. The little girl gasped loudly. "I love stories! Daddy reads them to me all the time!"

Silvia sighed and sat down on the swing next to the little girl. "I used to love them too, kid. Things change."

The girl looked down at her feet, the sadness returning to her composure. "Is it because of the park?"

Silvia laughed. "Yeah I guess."

The girl's shoulders shrunk. They both sat in silence. After a moment, the little girl sat up suddenly, gasping. "Well maybe then you and Daddy can make a book about it!"

Silvia laughed at her as she jumped from her seat.

"And then," the little girl stood, getting excited, raising one stubby finger to the air in triumph, "then if you make a book, we can sell it in a bookstore!"

Silvia smiled, and the girl continued. "Think about it! It really is a really nice park. Maybe if you write about it no one will ever forget about it!"

Silvia's expression went blank. She looked at the girl in awe.

"Yeah! Then everyone will know how wonderful the swings are! We can share them with everybody!" Suddenly serious, the girl walked in front of Silvia and stood with her face awkwardly close to Silvia's. "Will you write a book for me?"

Silvia didn't respond.

"Please?"

Silvia went to say something.

The girl stepped back and looked at her feet, solemnly. She almost whispered, "I really don't want to forget about the swings."

A Day at the Park

Not saying anything, Silvia looked at her. A feeling she had hardly ever felt in her life washed over her, and she suddenly felt anew. She rose and stared down at the girl, a concerned look on her face. It was as if nothing in the world were more important.

"Sure, I'll write you a book."

Instantly the girl's face lit up, and she covered the gasp escaping her mouth with both hands. "Really? Oh really? Will you?" The girl jumped up and down and squealed in a way that always annoyed Silvia the most. And yet, Silvia laughed. The girl jumped forwards and hugged Silvia around the hips, her huge smile squishing against Silvia's stomach. Silvia smiled, but lifted her arms away from her.

"You're the best!" The girl squeaked.

Then, Silvia heard a deep voice yelling at them from the distance. She looked up from the girl, and across the soccer field she saw a house where a large man was standing on the lit porch waving at them.

The girl gasped and looked up at the man, then quickly back at Silvia. "Oh! There's Daddy!" The girl broke free from Silvia. "Oh I can't wait to tell him! He'll be so happy!"

The girl began running across the field as fast as her scrawny legs could carry her. She turned back at Silvia and shouted, "Meet me at the park tomorrow, okay?"

The girl waited hopefully, and Silvia nodded. The girl bounced up and down, waved once, and ran across the field. Silvia waved until she disappeared into her house.

Silvia stood alone in the grey park, unmoving.

She half smiled to herself, thinking. She put her hands in her jacket pockets and sauntered slowly back towards the bench, kicking dirt up lazily with her feet as she went.

When she almost reached the grass, she felt something metal beneath her foot. She stepped backwards and knelt down, reaching for the shiny object beneath the soil. It was an old pen, scraped on the edges and barely colored. And yet, it was full of ink.

Elusive Childhood Dream

Fernando Yee

Childhood was often said to be the most innocent part of life. Children's brains were as squishy as play dough and the level of self-control was equivalent to a peanut – absolutely nutty. It wasn't like that mattered though. After all, what responsibilities were enlisted onto mindless children? That's right – nothing, other than the task of eating all the vegetables on the dinner plate. However, I was a super child. I would power through my vegetables, power sweep the floor and power clean my room. I knew I was different, and I felt other powers persuading me to partake in a different set of responsibilities than the usual "eat your vegetables" task. I was the chosen one, and I knew my fate was set. I was given the responsibility of becoming a ninja.

Elusive Childhood Dream

My eyes bulged out of my head as my mouth opened wide, jaw hitting the ground. There I was, a six year old child, obsessed with leg-crossing and television-watching. I observed in awe, my favourite morning television show, *Teenage Mutant Ninja Turtles*, where my most admired character, Raphael, would never cease to kick butt. His rebellious title and "I will destroy you" personality always hooked my interest. To top it all off, he had the best set of weapons – a pair of tridents. If I could be one ninja turtle, I would be Raphael, but knowing the trouble associated with a pair of tridents, I knew I should look into one of the brothers. Next I watched Donatello, observing his character. He looked exactly the same as his brothers, which was to be expected, but the purple headband radiated something, a sort of aura that seemed charming, peaceful and knowledgeable. Even better, his weapon was easily accessible. For several minutes, I scrounged around my house, looking for a replica of his apparatus. It wasn't long before I was ready to give up, but the sunlight caught something in the corner of the room. I slowly approached this mystical object, afraid of its powers. My hand slowly reached for the thin neck of this weapon. As I came in contact with it, I caressed the blunt edge, feeling the plastic caps that signified the end of the beating. One small hand movement and one huge leap for my progress. I raised this object above my head, holding it as if I was the master of combat.

It was then that my sister came barging down the stairs and took a good long look at me. She burst into laughing, mocking me for carrying a broomstick above my head.

Training had to begin soon. It started off with the sound of wood whipping aimlessly through air; typical for a beginner like me. I was no Donatello yet, but I knew I had to keep up and press on to become a ninja myself. The hours of swinging a broom handle translated into jelly arms. I spent the rest of my first training day resting on the couch, watching and analyzing reruns of the Teenage Mutant Ninja Turtle series. It was unfair. Unfair how Donatello gained his skill from being a pizza-eating, sewer-dwelling, mutant-changing turtle. Why couldn't I be so lucky? Why couldn't I be a turtle? It was then I had an epiphany. I didn't have a potion to turn me into a turtle, nor did I have the privilege of living in a dank sewer, but I did have the third vital component – leftover pizza in the fridge.

There was a guard protecting the entrances to the cold treasure trove; the perfect opportunity to test what I had learned during my first day of training. I skulked past the tables, crawling as if I were a cat. Stealthily, when the guard wasn't looking, I prowled towards the door to the treasure chest. The guard happened to leave the room, perhaps for a washroom break. This was it; it was now or never. I ripped open the door, and the yellow glow of the lights illuminated the various types of wealth inside the cave. Ignoring all the ordinary riches, I kept my eyes peeled for the prize. There it was, a golden box, stained with spots of grease, hiding behind the milk bags and eggs. I maneuvered my hand strategically and swiftly past the traps of milk and eggs, carefully picking the box and driving it towards myself. All of a sudden, I heard stomps walking towards me. I didn't have much time left. I had to work fast to prevail my mission. It took immense accuracy to close the door quickly without making a sound, but it was something I had already previously mastered through the art of racooning food in my earlier years. I easily slipped away behind the table, pizza box in hand. I made it out alive. I crawled out of the kitchen feeling like a true ninja. I had just survived sneaking past my mom for some leftover pizza.

I sat myself back down on my throne. My greedy hand shoved slice after slice into my mouth. It wasn't long before I felt a stomach ache arising inside me. There was one slice left, and I had to scarf it down to become a true ninja. I instantly regretted the pizza smorgasbord. I ran towards the washroom with my stomach ready to explode. All the pizza was dispelled out of my mouth, and I had lost all the powers I gained. I was never going to be a true ninja.

I woke the next morning feeling better. I was refreshed and ready for my second day of training. I reached to my side to grab my broomstick, only to feel that it was missing in action. I began to panic. Without my weapon, I was defenseless; in the movies, it's always the defenseless that get taken out first. I scrambled to my feet, forgetting my regular morning routine. I ran down the stairs, back to the sacred place where I first met with my weapon. There it was, in that very same corner where I first found it, with the identical shine of the sun reflecting off it. However, this time, the room was eerie, the walls were eerie, my emotions were eerie – everything was eerie. I approached the broomstick, only to find that it had been screwed into some heavy contraption that made the end feel abnormally heavy. I began to unscrew the damned contraption from my weapon. Abruptly, I heard something; loud footsteps were rapidly approaching. They were headed for me and they didn't sound welcoming. A loud roar pierced my ears, and I felt my soul draining just by listening to the horrid sound. After the howls settled, a quiet, drawled out whisper became apparent. "You are making a big mess," it breathed.

I was damned, doomed, done. The demon of the depths was before me, and there was no escape, no liberation, no chance. I tucked the weapon under my arms, fearing that swinging it around in these confined spaces would cause the walls to cave in on me. Time slowed down as my eyes scanned the surroundings for possible escapes. An oculus appeared right between the demon's legs, and with my legs compressed, I prepared for take-off. With blade-like precision, I surged through the opening, passing through the escape window effortlessly. I landed with a rolling summersault and sprung back onto my legs. "Come back here with that," the demon demanded me. I immediately left the emptiness and evilness behind me. As I bolted to my room, only echoes of the demon's cries caught up to me. It was a close call, but I survived my second mission. I survived the wrath of my dad.

I clambered back onto my bed breathlessly. The duty

of a ninja was much too burdening for me. I felt encouragement being emanated from the broomstick, but I concluded that it was the beginning of insanity. I sat up in my bed, observing the broomstick. I rolled the weapon between my palms, feeling the imaginary metal accents embedded into the wood. I questioned whether the life of a ninja was worth the risk and dangers that lay ahead.

"Go, go, Power Rangers!" The screech of an alarm clock excited me. My head snapped towards the sound to focus on the noise source; a red Power Ranger posed with legs in a wide stance, one hand on his hip and the other arm pointing straight up, fist clenched heroically. My eyes studied the plastic figure, curious about its character. All of a sudden, my eyes widened with adventure. Being a ninja was marvelous, but a Power Ranger could easily overpower a ninja. Swiping the broomstick off my bed and onto the ground, I stood up, posed in a fighting stance. I made the conscious decision to retire from being a ninja. It was time to embark on my journey as a Power Ranger.

Diplomacy

Chris Nesbitt

Ignus deVanderall of the Brotherhood of All Men sat with his fellows around the long oak table in the great hall. The tension in the room was thick as the tobacco smoke that hung in the air; hushed voices wound around the room in whispers, leaving an anxious edge as they travelled. The men had come to fix relations, which was much like patching holes in a man fresh from standing in front of a firing squad. For Ignus' party was not alone at the table; at the opposite end of the table, lay the other dignitaries and his fellow ambassador, a Thomas Hardwell of the United Thanian Confederacy, who was currently paying close attention to the grain of the table. DeVanderall calmly rose from his seat.

Diplomacy

DeVanderall stood out among his fellows, wearing long, close fitting robes, adorned with his emblem, a scale made of swords balanced by a man and a stack of coin on each side. His head was shaven, as was tradition, and he wore a light tan cowl in such a way that his tattoos were glimpsed at the edges as a reminder of his status. He folded his bracer-covered hands and held them in front of his mouth. He quietly sighed and made his hands into fists, holding them against one another by his sternum, as if to signal a request for quiet. Hardwell watched closely; this was the first thing he'd done since they began well over an hour ago, and the table quieted down in recognition, tense and curious.

The moment that silence fell in the great hall, deVanderall lowered both of his fists to the table with a heavy thud, rattling the china on the table much like the men's core and held still, with regal form. He took another breath, and out came an aggravated sigh from Hardwell, who held up his head with his hand and looked down at his cup, stirring it lazily. His attention proving harder to draw than borders.

"Is there a problem, Mr. Hardwell?' deVanderall inquired sarcastically.

Hardwell continued to look down and stir the contents of his cup. It had gone cold long ago, but it was the most productive thing he'd done today, so why stop now?

"You are fully aware as to why we are all gathered, yes? You understand why we've chosen to be here?" he pressed coldly, raising his eyebrows.

48

"Yes, I do…" Hardwell snapped, sitting up stiffly with resting his elbows on the table, and sliding his cup aside. "….and I don't need your reminder," he finished assertively. DeVanderall sat unperturbed onto his chair, as his opposite stood.

Hardwell rested his hands on his lapels, and pushed out his chest with a breath, growing a lion's mane. "Our great nations, as we all know, come from the same roots. Both our nations were born from the ashes of the aristocracies from the Sea of States, overthrown by the same movement, under the same ideals and with the same hopes." DeVanderall rolled his eyes and gazed up at the ornate chandeliers hanging above the table. It seemed Thomas had pulled out the valiant speech this time

Hardwell's voice rose with practiced enthusiasm: "And it seemed as though those crumbled States would band together to forge a new world power, a commonwealth of independent nations that would rise and soar." He reached into the air above him, as his emphatic voice shifted tone, "But alas there was divide, there were others that –"

"That what Mr. Hardwell?" deVanderall's voice echoed down the somber table.

Hardwell paused to take a breath, "That wished," he corrected reluctantly, "to allow all people their say in the nation's affairs."

The two men stood fixed, staring at one another as if the other would drop dead if they willed it hard enough. The others, who had been silently watched the two men bicker like children over a line in the sand, now watched intently, through the haze of smoke and sweat that strained their vision. The bald priest had drawn blood, and they could all smell it.

"A desire that the Confederacy fulfilled," Hardwell spoke up.

"In a sense," deVanderall replied nonchalantly.

"There was also the issue of everyone being entitled to the sweat of their brow and the strength of their back."

"As everyone should."

"Without having to give upwards of seventy-five percent," retorted Hardwell.

"An openly accepted and willfully given tribute."

And with that, both men ran out of steam, the last of their energies puttered away with this last bout. Hardwell slid his cup over, looking thoughtfully into it as he swished its contents and drank deeply. DeVanderall reached up to his neck and began to remove his cowl, revealing his bald tattooed head. He patted the sweat from his face. Both enervated men looked up and began to laugh. It was the first time one had seen the other so tired. The room seemed vivacious for that fleeting moment, and it seemed that everyone had a grin of some description stretched across their face.

"We could really carry on like this for some time couldn't we?" said DeVanderall, stifling a low chuckle with the back of a hand, as he re-wrapped his cowl.

Hardwell wiped his lip with his thumb and lowered his hands to his hips, "That we could…we could indeed." Hardwell looked down and stared at the table.

All the men began collecting the various folders and papers from the table, muttering to one another and exchanging pleasantries, while the only men who mattered dared not look each other in the eye.

"It's time then. I suppose it was only inevitable, but I must admit that I held out the smallest hope for the unthinkable," DeVanderall said, the laughter fading from his voice.

"We all did," said Hardwell. He raised his head to look at all the other men who now waited patiently behind their chairs.

"I want to hear you say it," deVanderall said firmly.

"Say what?" Hardwell said, perplexed.

DeVanderall grinned: "You're a diplomat, and you're the representative not just of your policy, but of your people…" he said, his voice filling with exasperation "…I want to hear you say it so I know that there's more at stake here than just the pride of two nations and their plated crowns."

Hardwell sighed, rested a hand on his forehead, and collected what little energy he had left In a weak fluttery voice, he said, "Zealot…"

deVanderall stood staring at Hardwell for the longest time. Then, stately as ever, he bowed and marched away, his delegation in tow.

Diplomacy

After the opposing delegation had left the room, Hardwell took a deep breath – doing his very best to keep his overwhelming disappointment in check. He stood in front of the men who'd served as his delegation. "Alright, you all know what to do. Send word to Ridgemount. The conference has failed, and this evening marks the beginning of war...against a foe who need not have existed." Then Hardwell turned and marched from the room, before he needed to waste more of his precious words and conscientious breath on covered ears and the barrels of loaded guns.

GRADES 9 - 10

White Rose

Ellen Zhang

It had been a year.

A year since they had last seen each other.

Riko woke up. She blinked, waiting for her vision to clear before making her way out of her room. Yawning she dragged herself to the kitchen. She smiled softly at the white roses that adorned the window sill. Reaching out, she picked one from the vase and placed it carefully under her nose.

That's the one I'll bring today.

Riko took a quick shower and then bundled herself up to prepare for the cold weather outside. She needed a walk. She could use the fresh air.

She swiped open her phone, smiling down at the message. Turning on the speakerphone, she let the voice she loved cut through the tormenting silence that enclosed her home.

Riko, heeey.
It's not important, I just, uh. Yeah, I'll see you in a little while, okay?

* * * * *

She stood shivering in the cold, carefully holding the white rose. The cold wind nipped at her skin. She inhaled deeply, an overwhelming sense of nerves suddenly washing over her.

It's been a year.

She cleared her throat, wanting to drown out the all too quiet atmosphere between them. "Hi baby," she greeted him, biting her lips, before they turned up into a small smile. "I got you this." She glanced at the white rose she held out. "Your favorite."

It was silent again.

⊠She shook her head, swallowing thickly before continuing.

"Remember when you first told me how much you loved these?" She twirled the rose between her fingers. "And I went on about how I hated them, but you told me to prove my undying love for you I'd have to keep them alive?" she laughed, her breath vaporizing in the air.

56

* * * * *

"How could you hate flowers?" Hiro asked, completely baffled by this new-found information.

"I just don't care for them." Riko shrugged. "I mean, okay, what? They're nice to look at. You take care of them for a while, and then what? They just wither away and die. They're pretty, and then they die. It's just pointless."

Hiro turned around, his face contorting in utter shock while the words spewed so casually from her mouth.

When she caught the sight of him, she laughed. "You're looking at me like I killed someone."

"I didn't know I was in love with such a heartless person."

"Shut up." Riko playfully pushed him. "I'm capable of love, okay? Just not with flowers."

"Evil." Hiro shook his head. "Pure evil."

"I'm just saying…"

"Hey, humans are pretty, they wither away and eventually die. So, you're basically saying it's pointless to care for anything living?"

Riko nodded. "I'll take care of you as long as you're still pretty. When you begin to wither, you're on your own."

"You evil person."

⊠A certain batch of flowers suddenly caught Hiro's attention. He carefully traced his finger along the edge of a white rose petal.

"These are my favorite," he informed Riko. "Aren't they pretty?"

Riko bit her lips, stifling the laugh that threatened to escape her. She forced a nod. "Then that's it. It's official," Hiro declared. "The white rose is our flower, okay?"

"For now," Riko mumbled.

"Okay, you know what? You have to take care of it."

"No."

"Yes," Hiro ordered. "Just water it. Let it be pretty for as long as it can, to…to prove our undying love for each other."

Riko rolled her eyes. "It's gonna die eventually."

"I know." Hiro nodded. "Just like everything else, but in the meantime, keep it alive, for as long as you can."

Riko narrowed her eyes, studying her boyfriend. "You're so weird sometimes."

"I'm not the one who hates nature." He paused. "But will you do that for me?"

Riko's expression softened, the almost pleading tone to his voice taking her aback slightly. "Of course…" she reassured him.

* * * * *

"Then you eventually asked me if my mind had changed. If I still hated flowers 'with a passion.' " She smiled. "Well, it did. I love them now…They're all over the house," she continued. "I always take care of them, keep them pretty until they…"

She blinked. "…until they wither away and die…" Like everything else.

She cleared her throat, shaking her head in order to rid the thoughts currently consuming her. "A year, a whole damn year. Has it really been that long? Where did the time go?"

She carefully examined the rose she had been holding.

"I've missed you." Her voice was soft, barely above a whisper, "I love you…"

She trailed off, unable to find her voice in the moment. It's been a year and I still love you.

* * * * *

"It's been a year, a full year. Where'd the time go?" A man's voice traveled to her, and Riko smiled, shaking her head lightly.

"Five years," she replied. "Tomorrow, it'll be our fifth anniversary."

* * * * *

"I miss him." Riko's words were soft.

Sora felt his eyes glisten with tears as they trailed along the headstone before him. He turned his attention to Riko, who was fixated on the rose she had placed down carefully next to the grave.

Her tear-fogged vision was still focused on the rose. "I told him to go," she admitted suddenly.

"What?" Sora questioned, turning his attention to the teary-eyed woman next to him.

"I told him to go," Riko repeated. "To leave that night."

"Riko, don't do this –"

"I need to," she cut Sora off. "It's killing me. I haven't said it out loud yet. I need to."

She inhaled deeply, her fingers clenching into a fist. The memories of that painful night flashed in her mind. They were always there, either in the front or back, constantly, and it took all she had not to focus directly on them.

"I told him to go. The night before our fourth, I told him to go, take care of what he needed to because I wanted him home the next day, the whole day, no excuses."

Sora closed his eyes, avoiding the pain that was apparent on Riko's face. He exhaled sharply, all the while running his hand up and down her back, silently urging her to let it all out.

"He was gone when I woke up," Riko began again. "I did some things around the house, I showered, came back and had a new message…from him."

Riko pulled out her phone –

Riko, heeey.
It's not important, I just, uh. Yeah, I'll see you in a little while, okay?

The message played, the two listeners lost within the familiar voice they had the pleasure of hearing for years while the trio were the closest of friends.

"I haven't heard his voice...for so long."

Riko closed her eyes to keep the tears back. "I was just about to delete it when..." She paused. "...when I got the call."

* * * * *

Riko trudged through the doorway of her empty house, clutching a vase that held a single flower. She placed it down on the table, along with a letter from Hiro that had been retrieved from the accident. She rubbed her aching head, her tired eyes and glanced over at the clock.

⌧12:17 a.m.

Her eyes landed on the letter, "Happy anniversary."

* * * * *

"What are you going to do tomorrow?" Sora asked.

Riko glanced around, eyeing the cemetery in the distance. "I'll be here." She smiled. "By his side, just like the last four times."

* * * * *

Riko curled up comfortably on her side of the bed. She glanced at the clock. It was now past midnight. "Happy fifth, Hiro," she whispered softly into the still air before reaching over and shutting off the light on her bedside table.

* * * * *

Riko woke up, a grin spreading on her face the moment her eyes began to flutter open. Four years? Has it really been four years? She noticed a glass vase containing a white rose sitting on top of a letter bedside table.

She threw her legs over the bed, pulling the envelope out from underneath the vase and shook her head lightly.

"He's so romantic."

To my one and only,

Hey, today's the day. Our fourth anniversary. Seriously, has it been that long? I've put up with you for that long, really? The things I do for love.

Anyway, I don't really know what to say that I haven't already. I love you, I've loved you for so long and I will always love you. The most special person I have ever met. The weirdest, funniest, prettiest – until you wither away and die, that is – and not to mention the most evil.

So, I got you your favorite flower, right? Because I know how much you love them. Well, to prove your love for me...you know where this is going. To prove your undying love for me, keep this white rose alive and pretty as long as you can.

I love you,

Your one and only, until I'm not pretty anymore,

Hiro

* * * * *

Riko's eyes shot open, running her hands through her hair before cupping her face. She wiped away the tears that had fallen. Her heart pounded harshly in her chest, her body coated with sweat. She let out a deep sigh, glanced at her bedside table, smiling before grabbing the letter. Each morning, she would read it, each morning tears would drop on the cream-colored note, yet it remained intact. She slid the letter back in the envelope. She smiled, patting the empty space on the bed next to her. "Happy sixth, Hiro."

* * * * *

Sometimes called "the flower of light", one of the meanings of white roses is everlasting love – love stronger than death, an eternal love, undying and all sustaining. They can symbolize new beginnings, or be a sign of farewell.

The Soulmate Clock

Alexa Jacob

There is a place,
Deep underground,
Where people hide things,
That they don't want found.
Full of dark thoughts,
And broken dreams,
Dark things stir,
Though ordinary they seem.
You wouldn't be able to tell,
At first glance, what they hide,
But as the clock keeps ticking,
Less time they will have to abide.
When the clocks all chime as one,
The nightmare will have then begun.

The Soulmate Clock

The glass will break,
The demons will wake,
And every wrong will be replayed.

Beep. Beep. Beep.

The infernal sound of a Soulmate Clock going off jarred me from my book of poetry. I rolled my eyes, then waited for the overly excited screeches to ensue. I waited, but nothing happened. The beeping merely continued. Confused, I looked around, but there was no one there. Then I froze. It couldn't be…could it? Slowly, I looked down at my own wrist. I gasped.

"No." I whispered. That wasn't possible. Ten minutes. That's all the time I had. The band that had been embedded in my wrist since birth flashed twice and then the countdown began. I was terrified, but the countdown didn't stop. I was going to meet the one.

Nine minutes. I was hiding in the poetry section at the back of the library. It was the only place that I could really find quiet. I came here every day after class to study and read. I came to be alone. Why did it have to be here?

Eight minutes. I stood up and brushed the dust off of my jeans. That was the only problem with the old books that I loved – the dust. I sneezed as it filled the air.

Seven minutes. Why did it have to be here? This section of the library was the only place in the world where I could be alone. Sure, the fact that everyone was now able to know exactly when they met their soul mate meant that the world was a wonderful place, nothing like what they taught us about in history, but a person still wants to be alone sometimes. As Shakespeare so brilliantly wrote, "My library was dukedom large enough."

Six minutes. Five minutes. Four. I didn't know what to do. What was I supposed to do? How do you prepare for something like this? How do you ready yourself to meet your other half?

Three minutes. My heart was racing. I began to put my books away. I didn't know what else to do. The pile was huge. I could hardly see where I was going. I made my way down the rows. I re-shelved Shakespeare and Edgar Allen Poe, Robert Frost and Emily Dickinson, anthologies of famous poetry, plays, and novels. Then a thought hit me…what if my soulmate didn't like books?

Three minutes, thirty seconds. Of course, that was absurd. We were going to meet in a library. But then again, that didn't mean anything.

Two more minutes. All of the books in the world could never have prepared me for today.

One minute. I was getting so nervous I wanted to sink into the floor.

Thirty seconds. What was going to happen?

Fifteen. What if they hated me?

Ten. What if I hated them?

Nine. I can do this.

Eight. Breathe.

Seven. Stay calm.

Six. Breathe.
Five. Don't freak out.
Four. Breathe.
Three. Stop hyperventilating.
Two. Breathe.
One. I bent my head around to look at the watch on my wrist. The numbers faded. Wait…that meant…

All of a sudden I was crashing to the floor. My books scattered everywhere. I looked up, ready to apologise to whomever I had walked into, when my green eyes met grey ones. My eyes widened. I smiled, and then took the hand that reached out to me.

"Hello," I said quietly, unsure how to react.

"Hey." His voice was deep as he helped me stand up. I bent down to begin picking up the many novels that had scattered across the floor. He stooped down as well.

"So, have you read a lot of Shakespeare?" he asked as he picked up the well worn copy of *Hamlet* that I had read countless times before.

"Yes," I replied, defensive. It wasn't uncommon for other students to ridicule me for my preferred reading material.

"For this relief much thanks. 'Tis bitter cold, and I am sick at heart," he quoted.

It was at that point that my opinion began to change; maybe the Soulmate Clocks weren't such a terrible idea after all. As Shakespeare wrote: "Doubt thou the stars are fire, Doubt that the sun doth move, Doubt truth to be a liar, But never doubt I love."

A Basket Of Love

Kerri Benallick

I always heard my grandfather talking about the "Good old days," and how everything was so much simpler back then. Now we have all these fancy gadgets, and high tech computers. I thought that it was a good thing that technology is more advanced. Now, I realize what he means. Simple. Simple things are sometimes the best things. Especially when it comes to love.

There weren't a lot of things that confused me. You know, being a fifteen year old genius and all. But there was something that I never really understood. Love. So many people had so many different definitions and interpretations of it, so I never really knew what it truly meant. It was that day, sitting on the old wooden swing on my great aunt Linda's front porch, that I found out what true love was.

A Basket Of Love

We were drinking our fresh lemonade, when she had said that she wanted to show me a photo album, She was gone for about two minutes, when she came out with an aged wicker basket, and a tear in her eye.

"Did I ever tell you the story of great uncle Andrew?"

I shook my head. She sat down beside me and looked down at the basket in her hands.

"It was 1944. The year before the second world war ended. He was one of the first to volunteer that year. I had begged him for days to stay, but by the time he had to leave, I knew I had to let him go. I was terrified for him. The only thing that made me go on were the letters we sent back and forth. I got one...maybe once a week. In one of his letters, he promised that he would bring me back a basket of Dutch tulips, as there were beautiful ones that grew near where his troop was set up. After about seven months, there were less and less letters, and eventually, they stopped coming. I sent letter after letter, hoping that I would get a response back from at least one of them, but I never did. Twelve months in, I had lost all hope. One May morning, I found a box on my doorstep. The return address showed that it had come from Holland. I couldn't decide if I should be excited, or horrified, but I was preparing myself for the worst. I ripped open the box to reveal a lovely basket full of faded red tulips."

She stopped for a moment as the tears were flowing at a steady pace down her cheeks and landing right in the basket. I noticed now that there were almost white petals covering the bottom.

"I thought that that was a good sign, that throughout all his hard work and efforts to keep himself and his friends alive, he had remembered to get me the tulips. But then I saw the letters. All of the recent ones I had sent were in a neat pile tied up with some white string. Unopened. There was also an envelope taped to the side of the basket. It was addressed to me. From him. I ripped it open as fast as I could. I had started to read but stopped at the end of the first line."

She lifted up a small board of wood at the bottom of the basket to reveal a letter. THE letter. She slowly opened it and began to read.

To my Wife,

I hope you have received your tulips. I knew I couldn't go without retrieving them for you. It happened three days ago. I was walking to the tulip patch after I had snuck away, when I was shot in the upper thigh. I knew that if I was hurt bad enough, they would send me home, but I knew you love tulips so I dragged myself the rest of the way, filled up the basket, and slowly went back to the makeshift hospital. They told me that the bullet was deep, and it needed to be removed. All I was worried about was getting better. A day after, the doctor told me told me the bullet had caused an infection, and they hadn't treated it fast enough, and it was the end. Therefore, here I am writing to you one last time, and telling you that I

71

love you very much.

With Love,

Your Husband

My aunt took my hand in hers, looked straight in to my eyes. "And that, my darling, is what true love really is."

Aunt Linda stood up. She grabbed our empty glasses of lemonade and went back inside. She came out seconds later with the photo album that she had been looking for in the first place. She opened it up, and flipped to the back. There was probably a whole ten pages just for him.

Andrew Ethan Roberts. March 18th 1924 – May 9th 1945.

There were dozens of the Dutch tulip petals, beautifully arranged around his name and birthday. Following, were a series of photographs. There were several from their wedding day. One was of my second cousin Miranda. Their first and only child. The picture was dated just days before Andrew had left. She was smiling proudly in between her mother and father. Her expression suggested that she didn't have a care in the world. I smiled at that. Innocence. It was a wonderful thing. Then you realize that life isn't what it's thought out to be. It can't always be butterflies and rainbows. It's the simple things in life that make it wonderful.

Walking Away

Jassmeen Banger

The breeze gently blows through my hair as I slowly walk through the garden. I close my eyes, allowing the chilly wind to touch me. Opening my eyes I stare out into the distance, admiring the sun as it lowers itself into the hills. As I make my way to the wooden chair my hand accidentally brushes itself onto a thorn. Quickly taking my hand away I look to see if the thorn left any marks. My hand stings, but it's bearable. More bearable than what I had experienced in the past…

3 years ago

"Please, let me go!" I screamed.

Daniel twisted my arm around my back and pinned me against the wall. His eyes were bloodshot red from drinking, and he was looking for someone to take his anger out. Unfortunately that ended up being me and the helpless baby that I was eight months pregnant with.

"Please, Daniel. Let me go," I begged.

"Why should I Scarlet?" he growled. "I asked you to give me a boy, someone who could carry on the family name, but instead you give me this? A girl!"

I guess that was why he was so mad; I was having a girl instead of a boy. How in the world was this my fault? I didn't have any control over what gender the baby was going to be. Without any warning, Daniel flipped me onto my back, shooting indescribable pain into my stomach. Using his huge hands he crushed my tiny wrist in his palms. It wasn't long before I could feel the pain spread throughout my body. I loudly screamed in desperation, trying to break free but Daniel's grip was too strong.

"Where did we go wrong?" I whispered to myself.

We were so happy when we had first gotten married. The countless dreams and hopes we had sowed together were now gone. The only thing left between us was hatred and the dark.

"Why in the world did I ever get married to a worthless woman like you?" he barked.

I looked up at him with disgust. "You think I'm worthless? The problem isn't me. You're the problem. The fact is that you don't know how to take care of another human being!" I yelled, spitting at his face.

Daniel released me from his grip and looked at me with his piercing blue eyes. "No Scarlet, you're the problem!"

Before I could have answered he slapped me across the face, making my cheeks sting. The pain was unbearable and within a few seconds I lost consciousness.

The next thing I knew it was early in the morning. I placed my hand on my stomach, praying that the baby was okay. A minute passed before I finally felt a light kick from inside. I smiled to myself. She's still alive.

Using all the strength I had, I slowly pulled my aching body out of bed. I looked around and noticed that I wasn't in the master bedroom. Ignoring the dark bruises on my body I limped to the master bedroom, only to find Daniel passed out in the arms of another woman. My heart ached at the sight of him and his mistress. He slept quiet soundly, like nothing had happened the night before.

As tears streamed down my cheeks I made my way to the closet and took out my suitcase. I had tried leaving multiple times before, but Daniel always managed to convince me to stay. Today that would all change. After dropping the suitcase at the door I walked back into the master bedroom. Managing my way around the bed I limped to Daniel's side of the bed. Bending over, I leaned into Daniels face, admiring his light hawk hair that covered his eyelids.

I leaned a little closer and closed my eyes. "Goodbye, Daniel," I softly whispered, and with that I left the house never looking back.

Present

"Mommy!"

Startled, I look around to find Mable running towards me. I quickly wipe away the tears that were running down my cheeks. One thing I definitely don't regret is giving birth to Mable. The moment I saw her I knew that I wasn't alone; she filled the hole that Daniel had left. I won't lie, even though it's been three years, I sometimes think about him. I think about how things could have been better between us. The reality is that it could have gotten a lot worse if I stayed.

"Mommy," Mable says hugging me.

"Did you need something Mable?" I ask embracing her.

Mable looks at me for a moment and says, "Come play with me."

"Okay," I say smiling

Tugging my hand she leads me into our house.

Love is nurtured by the idea that both partners care for and respect one another. The moment someone crosses their boundaries and hurts the other person, the love starts to shatter into tiny pieces. No matter how much you love someone it's sometimes best to leave.

Pure Silver

Khloe Henderson

Each day after Mom died I felt like I was walking on glass. Life was excruciatingly painful. I got in trouble at school, a lot, and I was apparently spending "too much time in the dark for a 9 year old". This was according to my dad who took me to a therapist to "work through my problems". I only had one problem and I didn't need some stranger to tell me what it was: my mother had died. I felt as if the words were burned into my eyelids. I would never be able to move on.

To please my father, I went to therapy for a while. It didn't help so Dad said I should take up a sport. I was drawn to archery. I loved it, and I became very good. I felt as if with every notch of the arrow I was launching my pain away from me.

Dad and I never talked about Mom, ever. She just lingered in the corners of our minds like a forgotten dream. He never told me what happened to her. I remember "accident" coming up a few times, but, my mother dying had been no accident. In the end, it was her kindness and bravery that got her killed and it would be those same things that would save me.

* * * * *

My father and I sat together at the kitchen table. Almost seven years had passed and it still felt empty without Mom. Her chair remained, as did her place, with neither of us having the heart to remove it. The anniversary – you could call it – of my mother's death was coming up. It was nine o'clock. We ate chicken and broccoli.

"How was work?" I asked, trying to engage in a conversation.

"Fine, Ezra," he replied in a monotone voice.

We didn't really talk a lot, not like before. Deep down, I felt as if my father had come to despise me. I reminded him of Mom too much, my turquoise eyes and long, thick, black hair just like hers. We finished dinner; I did my piano scales, and then made my way upstairs to bed. I popped into my father's room and kissed him on the forehead, before turning in myself.

I don't usually dream, but when I do, it has meaning. That night, I dreamt of my mother. I awoke to the sound of her sweet singing. I opened my eyes to see a white room. I was dressed in a cyan coloured, linen flowing dress and my mom was steps away. I ran to her and I could smell her sweet scent as she held me in her arms.

"My beautiful daughter, how I miss you." She pushed my long black hair out of my eyes. I smiled and snuggled closer. How I missed these hugs.

She wiped her wet eyes, "Ezra, you must listen to me. They're coming for you. They were not aware of your existence and now they consider you the same threat I was. They will do anything to stop our legacy."

I looked at her, dumbfounded. "What are you talking about?"

"Look, Ez, I don't have much time. When I was younger, I was part of a coven of witches. Our legacy was to be kind and brave; to help those who could not help themselves. My best friends: Sophia, Erin, Alison and Celestia slowly forgot the legacy they swore to uphold and one by one they turned to the dark side. They tried to pull me over as well, but I ran. I got away. I used my power for good, but always feared they would find me."

"Then they did," I said, digging my black painted nails into the palms of my hands. "That's why you died."

"Yes, they found me, they became angry and we fought. At the time, they didn't know of you, but now I fear they're coming for you as well." She looked around, like someone was watching.

"They're here," she said. "Remember, be kind, and be brave."

As my mother spoke, so many questions swam in my mind. Then, my dream shattered like glass as the shouts of my father tore me from sleep and my Mother's voice echoed in my head one last time: "You will know what to do. When you need it, it will be there."

As I whipped my covers off and jumped out of bed, I understood her message. I was the descendant of witches and it was up to me to protect the legacy. But, I had no idea how to control or activate my powers. My mother's words came back to me, "When you need it, it will be there." And right then, I needed it to save my father and avenge my mother.

A flash of light lasting a split second let me know my time had come. Not a moment later, I ran out of my bedroom and into my father's room.

The last thing I saw as I reached the door was a black figure pulling him out the window. Without hesitation, I ran down the stairs and into the garage. I pulled on my leather jacket and slipped on my black converse.

I grabbed my bow and quiver. I slung it over my shoulder and ran to my father's motorbike, grabbed my purple helmet and revved the engine. I opened the garage and flew down the street. I spotted the figure overhead and followed it for a good fifteen minutes until it lead me to the end of a road. I jumped off and ran after it through the forest. I scavenged my brain for ways to defeat demonic witches. I remembered, when I was younger, I read you could defeat a witch with fire or silver. I reached back and grabbed a plain, carbon fiber arrow and watched, in awe, as my touch turned it to silver. Years of hoping and wishing my mother was with me again crystallized in that moment, and I knew she was right next to me, smiling and proud. My powers had come to me, because I needed them, just like she said. I notched my arrow, ready to aim and fire at the first sight of movement.

Out of the corner of my eye I saw a streak of black in the dimming sun. I fired. A shimmering streak shot through the air, and as it did, a flame ignited at the tip. I heard a blood-curdling scream and realized I hit one! The witch disintegrated into a pile of mustard green dust and blew away. Two more came at me, throwing black fire. I swatted them away with a swoosh of my hand. My arrows met them as targets, leaving behind more piles of dust. I frantically looked for my father.

As I reached a clearing, I saw him, tied against a gnarled tree. I jumped as I dodged a ball of black fire. I got up, dazed, to see a woman dressed in black with long blonde hair, hovering above.

"Daughter of Margo," she said.

"And you are?" I questioned fiercely.

She laughed, a raspy laugh. "I'm surprised she didn't tell you. I'm Celestia and I'm the reason your good little mommy isn't here." She bowed and sneered.

"Look, I just came here for my dad, nothing else." – I lied

– "Just give him here and I can go," I demanded, getting angry and pointing at my dad.

"Not so fast, hun," she stated. "I'm not quite done with your family yet." I could see the beginning of a black fireball playing around her fingertips in the dim moonlight.

"You've already taken everything from me, no more!" I yelled. It echoed off the trees. I whipped an arrow out of my quiver and aimed. She laughed again.

"What is a little arrow going to do to me?" she cackled menacingly, throwing her head back.

I focused and watched as the carbon fiber changed to pure silver. I saw the panic rise in her face, but she concealed it quickly.

"So, you're magical too? I guess I'm just going to have to burn you first." The fireball around her fingers glowed ominously. I held my stance; for me, for Mom…for our legacy.

She raised a hand over her head and blasted me with balls of black fire. Each missed me in turn. As one flew at my face I released my shot. It burst though the black fire and ignited with teal flame. My arrow met its mark; Celestia caught fire and disintegrated into a pile of black ash. I walked toward my father and pulled him loose.

"Ezra!" he was speechless. I hugged him for a while, and, for a second, I could smell my mother's sweet scent.

I walked over to the smoldering pile of ash, knelt down and opened my palm; a black box appeared. I scooped up the remains of Celestia, locked the box, closed my eyes and pitched it into the forest.

* * * * *

Two days later, I went to visit my mom. As I knelt in the moist dirt, tears fell from my eyes as I told her, "It's all over mom, I did it. Our legacy lives on. Don't worry about those witches, they won't bother us again. Bravery and kindness always wins."

I closed my eyes and smiled. I could almost feel her arms holding me and her kiss on my forehead.

The Taming of The Wereshrew

Jordan Waverman

Our story starts on a spooky road, on a foggy night (as all stories must). A car drives down the road, the family inside completely oblivious to the sacrificial role they will play. The couple is talking in a quiet voice, hoping not to disturb their sleeping toddler, when they hit something. The husband curses, stopping the car, sure he has hit an animal. As he climbs out (rather unwisely; clearly he's new to the authorial business), he motions for his wife to find a flashlight.

As his wife leaves the car, flashlight in hand, she hears a gasp. "Honey?" she calls. No answer. She turns on the flashlight just as his corpse flies into her.

* * * * *

Sergeant Felix D'Esterly stared at the gruesome scene without batting an eye, unperturbed. Then he vomited. "What the bloody heck did this?" he cursed.

An officer answered him. "Well, it wasn't an animal, too neat. Our guess is cult, because of the symbols, and the similarity to the other one."

Sergeant D'Esterly looked at the sight, disgust on his face. He surveyed the road. The car had been bashed to pieces. What was once an unsuspecting couple was now merely blood on the ground. A few stomach wrenching symbols had been drawn in the blood. "And what of the child?" he asked. There were only a few bones in the back seat.

"Consumption."

The sergeant almost disgorged again. He wished he hadn't had spicy meatballs and beans for lunch. "Fair. This sounds like a job for Joe Andronicus, the best paranormal investigator in Canada!"

The officer winced. "This corpse is Joe."

Felix groaned. "Then call Murphy Ottern, the second-best paranormal investigator in Canada!" And with that, D'Esterly's poor stomach gave in, and he became culpable of the crime of destroying evidence.

When the second-best paranormal investigator in the country (or best, because Joe's gone?) arrived in his usual manner, he created little stir. In fact, no one even noticed him till he was examining the corpses, and even then he looked so right in this setting that no one cared until he started taking photos with his camera (none of this phone crap; horrible pictures).

Sergeant Felix hurried over. "Afternoon. Any thoughts?"

Ottern looked at him then, his drowsy gaze murkily concealing his thoughts. He glanced up. "Yes, it is." And with that, he pulled on a pair of gloves and began poking around.

Felix cleared his throat, saying, "I suppose you're wondering why we'd call you for this, when the police could easily handle it…"

"Not really," Murphy interjected, drawing Felix's ire. The detective plucked a piece of metal from the road, studied it, then placed it into a pocket. "Hmm…Osmium. But to answer your unspoken question, I am aware of why you hired me because of reasonable conclusions. Joe Andronicus was no lightweight when it came to safety, and if this car carried his son, then it was defended. And as you can see, it's destroyed. And after his mother last week…An easy case of reasonable conclusions, I'm afraid." Ottern knelt to examine a destroyed car door. "And by the way, I also know that this case can not be 'easily handled' by the police. No fingerprints, no weapon – just claw marks – symbols, magical burns throughout the car, and the fact that Andronicus removed the cults long ago…No, it would be too much trouble for you even to identify someone, nevermind catch them. That's why I was called in."

Felix looked ready to burst, but something stopped him.

"Hold on…No weapon? You mean this wasn't the work of a blast weapon? I'd have thought the magical burns would support that theory."

Ottern looked up at this, an expression of amusement flickering across his face. "Just why I was called in." Then he stood up, remarked his goodbyes and left.

Felix sighed, then looked at the door. He observed the rents in the sides, almost like claws instead of shrapnel, and shivered. He realized just why Ottern had laughed.

Delores sat inside the car, waiting. Murphy emerged from the forest, and stood there for three minutes before she noticed him. "Well? Any good?"

Murphy shrugged. "The cops in charge of this case are imbeciles. They think they're dealing with some variety of bazooka-wielding would-be-sorcerers. Found some good evidence, though." Murphy got into the passenger seat.

"Where to?"

Murphy considered this for some moments, then pulled out a chunk of Osmium.

Delores started at what Murphy held. "Powerful cult then?"

Murphy sighed. "I'd hoped I'd trained you better. What group uses Osmium in this joint? None of them are powerful enough. What was the first lesson of investigating?"

Delores sighed. "Always explore the layout of a town before you make your move."

Murphy smiled. "Good. Glad to see you've learnt something. Head for the shady town. We're looking for an unassuming building. Joe would have missed it; he liked his foes to be big and public."

Delores frowned as she drove. "Hold on. Are you saying that the person who killed the great Andronicus wasn't his foe? What happened down that road, then?"

Murphy grinned, flashed her the Osmium. "You'll see."

Delores groaned, sure that another session on reason was coming. Instead, she drove in circles for a half-hour before Murphy stopped her. He pointed to a brown building with boarded-up windows. Delores went to ask a question, but Ottern shushed her. They snuck out of the car, none of the passersby giving them any thought (as was usual when concerning Ottern), and slithered along the wall. When they reached the front door, Murphy straightened up.

"What? I thought we were supposed to remain silent and hidden?" Delores asked, irate.

Murphy shook his head. "No, we didn't have to. I just asked you to because every good detective story needs a scene where people sneak."

"Huh?!" exclaimed Delores. But Murphy was silent. He went to the door and knocked loudly. Delores was confused. "Why are we knocking? Shouldn't we sneak in, if we want a good...scene?"

Detective Ottern shook his head. "Tell me, have you ever heard of the Yakarzın Kitap?"

Delores nodded. "Weren't they some wackos who believed that we all lived in a story?"

Murphy breathed out, relieved. "Glad to see you recognize them. The Yakarzın Kitap, or The Author's Book, believe that life is some book written by an author and think that they are plot points in this story. Completely nuts, but deadly."

"Then why have we knocked on their door?"

"Because you never beat the Yakarzın Kitap unless they want you to. Most people aren't even aware they exist."

Delores stumbled backwards in shock. "You mean they lose intentionally? And how do you know it's them?"

At that point the door opened, and Murphy strode inside. He stood in the hall alone, looked around, and waited. "So many questions. Good. I know it's them because of REASON. Their symbol had been printed in the ground thirteen times in blood, and other groups aren't suicidal enough to use that symbol. Don't know why Joe didn't guess it was them after the first case, actually. They're the only people who provoke investigators of his status intentionally. And they often lose intentionally. They claim it's all part of the plot." No one appeared, so Murphy began to walk in the direction of the light.

Delores followed. "So if they sometimes win, shouldn't we be more careful?"

"Don't be ludicrous. Everyone wins sometimes." They emerged into a room. Thirteen people in cultist robes stood around a pentagram chanting. Murphy walked right up to the edge of the circle, no one noticing. Confident at the sight of Murphy standing there, Delores entered the room, forgetting that no one ever noticed Ottern.

"Intruders!" A man in black screeched, and the call was taken up. Then their chant changed suddenly. They began repetitively chanting, "Soricidae!" over and over.

Murphy stepped back for a moment, contemplation on his face. Then he opened his pocket, drawing out a night stick. He motioned for Delores to draw her own club. She hurriedly did so, glad that Murphy had given it to her. Murphy grinned once, then bashed a man with his. The chanting abruptly stopped. The cultists stared at Murphy for a moment (except for the one on the floor; despite appearances, Murphy had a strong arm), then one stepped forward. He removed his hood, staring at the detectives. A female to the side suddenly rushed forward, slitting his throat. He collapsed to the floor, symbols glowing, as all of the Yakarzın Kitap fled through a back door, chanting "Soricidae".

Delores moved to chase them, but Murphy stopped her. "No worry, I told a cop during the earlier scene where they'd be. We have another problem." He looked at the writhing cultist on the floor, who was beginning to shrink. "What do you think killed Joe?"

The man had stopped shrinking, and bore a shrewlike look. "A Wereshrew," stated Murphy. "Or that's what they call it. Technically it's an Elephant Shrew, which isn't a true shrew, but who cares?"

The small not-shrew stared at them, ready to pounce. Murphy nonchalantly pulled his phone from his pocket, and dropped it into the blood. The shrew was fried instantly, electricity overwhelming its tiny body. Murphy looked at Delores' shocked face.

"What? It wasn't a werewolf!"

Murphy turned and left the way he'd come, to the sound of police sirens and the uncaringness of a population.

Delores wasn't upset he'd left. He'd call her.

Markus stood in an alleyway, loitering. Murphy rounded the corner. "Evening, Markus. The plot of the author advances."

Markus nodded. "So it does…"

Dear Anne

Pooja Sankar

It wasn't supposed to be this way. Every birthday should be a happy, cheerful one. As twelve year olds, we dream, laugh and ponder. Many of the things we fantasize about are unknown, mystical, imaginary ideas that bring smiles to our faces. We think about ponies, puppets, rainbows and the greatest of friends. As twelve year olds, we don't wonder too much about the lives of others, we focus all too much on ourselves. The only thing rushing through Anne's mind as she sliced into the mark of her twelfth year of existence was, "Where could my Dad be, right now?"

As soon as Anne heard the last door close behind her, she knew it was time. She deserved an answer, now. She couldn't go another minute of another day with any more sorrow, desperation and neglect creeping in her veins. "Mom, where's Dad? How come he never came? Not once. I hoped that maybe today would be different. I try to reassure myself that I don't need him just like he doesn't need me, but I do. We could've been friends at least." Her face remained wet with woe as her chest kept heaving. "I thought he'd show up today. I pictured him hiding behind my friends, and I was going to run up to him and…Oh, I don't know what I would do if I saw him. Why does he hate us? Mom, tell me something, please!" Anne pleaded.

Ms. Lee's face was drenched with the waters of misery and blunt pain. "I do all this for you, and all you can do is think of your dad? He's never coming back for you, okay? Just for one day, why don't you quit it!" With that she paced upstairs, hiding her reddened, swollen eyes full of tears and despair.

Anne's mother loved her, cherished her, stood by her side, day and night, to take care of her. Her mother read her stories every night before bedtime that consisted of wild, exhilarating adventures. Anne was in awe, imagining herself flying, floating around the world seeking new explorations. Along with the fantasies and mythical adventures was never a story of a fun-loving, thrill-seeking man, her father. There wasn't one day where Anne didn't tug on her mother's woven dress pleading to know more. Every birthday, Anne had faith her father would return, from wherever he was, to sing to her. All she ever wanted was to pretend to be enraged on his return and then to say, "I forgive you, daddy," and give him the warmest, most sincere hug.

Questions about Anne's dad flustered Ms. Lee. Some days Anne found her mother on the porch with her head resting against the wooden fence, lamenting with a book at hand. Many people looked up to Ms. Lee, her mother. She always had plenty on her plate, but she made it all look too easy. When the sun lit up gold each morning, Ms. Lee would leave to work as long as she could, even on weekends, to make that extra penny.

On rare occasions, Anne got to visit granny. Most visits consisted of baking cookies and watching WW2 documentaries while grandma knitted her woolen, colourful scarves. Anne enjoyed the visits where they would bake red velvet cupcakes and talk about whatever filled their thoughts. If persuaded enough, her grandmother would sometimes recall stories of her son, Anne's father. Anne's eyes would twinkle hearing of a young boy with navy blue trousers running wild around town at midnight screaming, "I am free!" She would gaze up at the sky, stirring an imagination of what he could possibly look like now.

On Anne's 9th birthday, granny gave her a few words that meant more to her that any wrapped, expensive gift. Now, all Anne had of him was a poem, a ruffled sheet of paper that rested in the pockets of her worn-out navy blue overalls. It read:

I am free
Free as I could ever be
Free like the wind

Dear Anne

Or the oceans, sea to sea
In my skin, I am me
There is no greater feeling
Than the feeling of free

Anne felt exasperated. Her mother knew more that she was owning up to. She now sat alone on the cold hard ground picturing her father running wild in as cold and mysterious a night as this one. She looked out through her frosted windows to see the serenity of the silent cold, the midnight sky creeping upon her. The shadowy night hindered the moonlight that lead the way to her granny's. She threw on her beige winter coat, woolen mittens and draped on a velvety red shawl. A few subtle steps and a swift turn of the lock sideways was all it took for Anne's escape. It was only a fifteen minute walk to her grandmother's, but what made this a journey was the truth that was awaiting her arrival.

The night grew darker. Wolves howled. She wanted to be just like her father more than anything, running wild through the howling night, searching deep for the warmth of the midnight stars. There were no stars, no light and worst of all, no feeling of being free. She just felt alone. She couldn't turn back now. She kept after the indistinct yet familiar flicker of yellow, soon getting brighter and brighter. A bizarre sense of fear trickled down Anne's back as every step grew smaller and smaller. Suddenly, every moment spent thinking about her father all rushed back into her.

Every hope, dream, prayer, it all dashed back into her in-nocent, vulnerable self. Tears rushed down her cheeks for every single moment she ever felt neglected, forgotten or unwanted.

The flicker of yellow became a bright, newly-painted bungalow. Grandma Beatrice looked shocked to see Anne this late into the night, she rarely ever visited. The strange fact was that, even though they lived within a few kilome-ters of each other, Ms. Lee rarely took Anne to see her grand-mother.

Anne's frustrations with her mother grew. She buried her face deep into granny's worn out, grimy leather couch. Within a few minutes, Anne sat stooped, sighed in sorrow coming from deep within, and began. "I need to know now. Tell me everything. I'd much rather know the truth, no mat-ter how bitter it may be, than be drenched in imaginations of a fake reality, a brutal fantasy. Do you know how it feels to wake up every day asking yourself the same question but never, not even once, knowing what to tell yourself? I want to know how he feels right now. Maybe he's thinking of me today, just maybe."

Anne looked up to see that her grandmother was hold-ing a wrinkled sheet of paper clutched close to her heart and a silver necklace, engraved with the word, "Anne". She walked over, sat down, gazed deep into Anne's helpless blue eyes. "This is all that I have of him. He wanted me to give it to you on your 16th birthday." It read:

Dear Anne

My dear Anne,

At 16, an angel was sent for me. There's a woman who loved and cared for me, never knowing the love she deserved and needed. Life is not for hiding the most beautiful parts; it's about sharing those precious moments with the ones you love the most. I hadn't realized many things when you came into my life. The minute I left you, I could've turned back. I could've rushed back to your mother, and she would have had her arms open, waiting. She is the greatest woman. Never stop loving her. I know that sometimes it won't seem right, but when things go wrong, no matter what, she will watch out for you, every minute. There's plenty I want to say, but I know how easily teens get bored these days, so I'll keep this one short. Now listen carefully, sweet pea. I once thought that we were all born to run wild, run wild and free. I once thought isolating myself was the best kind of feeling. I was wrong. Don't you dare make the same mistake! The best kind of feeling is the one you get when you have someone there for you that you cannot imagine a life without. Tell your mother I love her. I will forever miss her, always. I'm sorry, my baby girl. I had to go. I'm sorry.

Love you to the moon and back,

Dad

"Grandma, where is he? Where's my dad? I have to

know now. I need to see him. Please, please tell me."

Her grandmother stood kneeling on the wall with a stack of old letters held tightly close to her heart, and tears gathering in her hopeless, withered eyes.

"Darling, this isn't easy for me to say, it will never be…" her grandmother began.

Be Good

Juli Docherty

Red.

All Aida could see when she closed her eyes was red. It was a deep shade, a colour that resembled blood. It was the last thing she saw before she found herself here, wherever here might be. And no matter how painful the fear was that the colour struck inside her, she would not open her eyes. She grew unsure of even grasping the ability to open them, because if she did, she knew she would see nothing but pitch black for what seemed like miles. It terrified her, both the pitch black and the red, but she would prefer the colour of blood than the unknown darkness that surrounded her.

There was no light in what she felt to be a room, a secured, locked up room. If there were windows, they were blacked out; the locked door, which she'd only seen once, blocked out the fluorescent lights that illuminated the mysterious room past the locked door.

Sometimes Aida wondered if she really is dead. If the black she sees is some sort of in-between state before the door opens and reveals the bright lights of Heaven, or perhaps the gates to Hell.

Aida wasn't a bad person, she just became involved with bad things and bad people. She knew those people would think of her to be rather inferior. Always there, but isolated and apathetic. But they never called her a bad person. They had always said she could carry the weight of others, but never once let anyone carry her own.

"It's too much of a burden for you to bear," she would say. "I'd rather carry yours than have you even think about mine."

As she sat in the dark, eyes still shut tight, she thought back on these things, these words people would use to define her. Who was Aida? She was a lonely girl who tried something, and got hooked on it. She never meant anyone harm, but she didn't need to go to the lengths she did to get what she needed. She didn't need to bust down the door of her house when her parents locked her out. She didn't need to steal her father's prestigious military medals and sell them to an antique dealer and drain their bank cards to get her the fix she needed. She didn't need to tell her older brother that it was only a phase, when she knew it was far worse. She didn't need to lie. That perhaps, was the worst thing she could have done to her family.

Though the words that they described her with were large in quantity, those people never said she was bad, nor good. It was almost as if she didn't belong in Heaven or Hell, perhaps just the in-between state she sits in now. Was there even a Heaven and Hell? Maybe there was only this, this pitch black. Wouldn't that be something, she snorted as she thought, everyone stuck in their own personal pitch black room. Then there was a part of her that thought she was already in Hell. She felt like she deserved it.

Aida couldn't remember how she ended up in this room, but she had an idea why. This was her judgement day. She thought back on her death, and the images of a gun, a masked man, and her brother, who was far better than she. He had offered, no, demanded, to take the bullet so that his sister could live and have a chance to get out of the horrible place she had let herself go to. Aida knew she didn't deserve it. She didn't deserve the gift her brother, only two years older, was whole-heartedly prepared to give her. His life, in exchange for hers. His life, in exchange for hers? No, he had always been so much better than she ever could. He could surely go farther in life with the goodness that rested inside him. It would be a waste of a life, in her opinion. She had nothing to lose, with the impurities she had put in her body, the drugs and alcohol were coming back to swallow her whole like a vicious monster, only it took on the form of a masked man with a gun, who demanded money she owed. Her brother was willing to die when he could live and do good to the world. What good had Aida done? She knew no one was going to leave that alley-way alive. He was too good, which is why she jumped in front of the bullet before it could touch him. She had absorbed the pain deep within her chest and stomach, crumpling to the ground like a rag-doll after the gunshots rang out. The man ran away, hearing police sirens in the distance, while Aida laid on the ground, dying in her brother's arms.

He held her head in his lap, brushing her raven-coloured hair away from the illuminating green eyes that had sunken, making her face look hollow. Tears welled up in his eyes as he shook his head. He blinked them away and stared at her wounds, knowing she wouldn't be saved in time. "Why did you do that?"

She smiled peacefully, grasping her brother's free hand with all the strength she had left. "Perhaps I'll be redeemed in Heaven, and be forgiven for all that I've done to you and the rest of our family. Be good, Isaac."

The last thing she saw was her brother's hand covered in her blood. It was the last thing she saw before her eyes became too heavy and shut, as if she were just falling asleep. She was left to her thoughts before her last breath escaped her, her final words echoing in her head. "'Be good,'" because she couldn't be.

She could only hope now that her brother was still good. She could never forgive herself if he ended up like her. If he became the same thing she had. Whatever she was, she decided, was not something she wished to see anyone, especially her brother, become. Maybe Hell was what waited for her on the other side of that locked door. She only hoped that what she had done might make her worthy to walk among the angels. Though, she knew her hopes were set too high.

Suddenly, bright lights filled the dark room as the locked door opened, revealing a woman with long black hair and tanned skin, sharing the same emerald eyes as Aida in a long white dress with wings fanning out behind her, pulling Aida from her memories. Then, Aida felt it, the weight of one thousand worlds being lifted from her shoulders.

The woman smiled serenely. "Hello, Aida." She held out her hands to the girl in the dark room. "It's time to go home."

GRADES 7 - 8

Morrow Well

Jamison Staines

The woods were quiet and peaceful, except for the crunch of leaves as a small boy walked across the earth. He glanced up at the trees and took a deep breath, inhaling the cold, autumn air. The sky was clear, and the leaves fell from the branches fluttering to the ground like vibrant orange butterflies. The trees below the valley looked like a wave of orange, all scattered along the branches. Overlooking this breathtaking sight was James Parker. James Parker loved adventure and hiking. He would wander the woods every day to clear his mind. He was an average height fellow, with short brown hair and a face full of freckles. His bold, daring nature made him, in most girls' opinion, a handsome young boy.

Morrow Well

As he was standing on the small hill, his peripheral vision caught something protruding from the grassy meadow below. He looked and saw a strange outline of bricks in the middle of the field. He couldn't see it from afar, but decided to investigate what it was, his curiosity getting the best of him. He climbed down the small rocky hill and sprinted across the field, the grass tickling his legs as they swayed in his path. He finally came closer to the mysterious brick pile; he looked hard at it and started to make out what it was. He stopped in front of it. It was a well. The bricks were old and covered with moss. The stones were cracked, showing the lines of age. He put his fingertips to the stone and felt the rough texture on his skin. On the top of the well was a rotting wood cover that was barely holding up. James eyes fell upon the wood cover and something caught his eye. On the cover, carved into the wood, were letters. James tried to read what the letters spelled.

"Morrow Well…What the heck does that mean?"

As James pondered over the strange words carved into the wood, he decided to open the cover and squatted to pull it up. His biceps tensed as he lifted the wood. He finally pushed the wood off and dust came flying out. He coughed and swatted it away. He lowered his head into the dark, damp hole. He couldn't see anything, but he smelled something rotting in the well. Probably the wood cover he thought. He looked into the ominous hole and stared into it, trying to see the bottom. He felt like he was staring into an empty abyss, the depth travelling far beyond his reach. It could be twenty feet, maybe even thirty. There was only one way to find out. He found a small dirty rock and dropped into the well. He imagined a splash noise, it seemed so real…then he realized he actually did hear a splash. He picked up another rock and watched it disappear into the darkness. He heard it splash into the icy black waters below. James wondered what he was going to do next. He still wanted to know what "Morrow Well" meant, and he knew exactly who would.

James called Kevin on his cell. He waited for Kevin to answer. Kevin Hills was probably doing his homework.

Kevin's voice came on. "James what do you want. I'm very busy."

"Dude, come to the forest where the valley is, you know, right beside the meadow."

"I believe I know where that is," stated Kevin.

"Okay, well anyways, I was just chill'n up on the hill when I found this sick well! It's so cool you gotta come check it out!"

"Perhaps I can." Kevin paused, and then the line went dead.

Kevin Hills showed up twenty minutes later on his bike. Kevin was one of the smartest people James knew. He always got good grades and never got in trouble. He was short. He was one of the shortest kids in his grade, and he got picked on for it. But James was always there to defend him. Kevin was a skinny boy with short blond cropped hair and glasses. Whenever his glasses would slip, he would always push the rims back up to his nose. Kevin moved cautiously to James. Kevin almost had a phobia of danger. He was the complete opposite of James. Anything that even mentioned danger, Kevin would be running far, far away. Finally, Kevin approached James after giving one more quick glance around.

"I'm not supposed to be out in the wood this far!" Kevin squeaked.

"Oh relax, bro. No one's out here! Now check this out!" exclaimed James.

Kevin slowly stepped toward the well, and looked deep into the blackness that surrounded the hole. Kevin looked fearfully at the well and his eyes came to the wood cover. His eyes swept over the words as he slowly mouthed each letter, putting his fingers to the wood, feeling the rough etches embedded into the plate.

"Morrow Well…" He pondered. "I believe that's an old English term meaning in the future…tomorrow." He looked up.

"Who would write Morrow Well on the cover of a well?"

Kevin made a face, the scrunched up confused face he would make whenever he was in the path of a problem. He crouched over the well trying to figure out what the heck "Morrow Well" was. Kevin stood up. James could tell that Kevin didn't like the well. He started to back away.

"I don't know about this James," stated Kevin. "I mean, it's not safe to just go jumping in a random hole. I know you haven't asked me if you want to go exploring the well yet, but knowing you, James...I...I know you want to do it." Kevin put his hands up in the air and started to jog back to his bike. James sighed. He knew Kevin wasn't up for it. Kevin never wanted to do anything fun.

"What a wuss." The anger in James' voice was apparent. He kicked at the dirt and watched Kevin bike away, disappearing into the distance. James sat by the well. He was just so curious about what was in the well he couldn't resist. It was like the urge of hunger. Slight, subtle pain. That was the same urge his gut told him to explore the well. But something was on his mind.

What if Kevin was right? Who knows what could be down there?

James decided that Kevin didn't know everything, and James didn't care what was going to happen. He stared at the well. He felt it calling to him. Beckoning him, as if it wanted him to come. He was going out that night.

* * * * *

It was the dead of night. James had snuck out of the house to go to the well. He was slightly scared, but his determination to go to the well was stronger than ever. The night sky was dark, except for the moon, pale and glowing. James reached the field and sprinted to the well. He stopped in front of it and picked up a rock. He dropped it down. There was no splash...no sound, as if the rock had disappeared into thin air. James grabbed a rope from his backpack and tied it tightly to the well. As he descended down the well, he started to smell something rotting and he coughed. He put his nose to his hoodie and held his breath. He felt his feet hit the bottom. He was starting to feel dizzy, and disoriented. Something misty was appearing in front of him. Before he blacked out, he noticed no water lay in the bottom of the well. Then, he fell back and a vision came to his eyes. He saw a shadowy figure lying in the icy waters of a creek, dead from drowning. James looked with horror when he came to, and he screamed. He fought nausea and dizziness as he scrambled up the rope and jumped out the well. He ran into the night, not looking back once.

The next day after school, James went hiking through the woods once more and stopped at the edge of the field. The well had gotten to him. He wouldn't dare tell anyone about the well. He took one last glance at it and backed away, heading home. As he stepped back he felt a rock slip from under his feet, and he tumbled back, hitting his head hard on the ground. He slipped into the creek behind him, unconscious. He fought at the black waters, and with his last breath he saw, from the corner of his eye, the well sitting in the field, almost watching him. It watched him die, watched him drown in the waters. James pushed and kicked until he lay still, floating in the water. Morrow Well sat in the field. Morrow. Future. Tomorrow. The well had shown James his fate. And Morrow Well had got what it wanted.

The Ocean

Luiza Aguilar

"I've always loved the ocean.

The way its waves wash up to shore tediously, one after another. The way the salt water is the home of countless creatures, giving up its freedom for the lives of others. The way you can just lie in the water for hours, drifting farther away from the loss and destruction that is life with each passing moment. The ocean is, to me, one of the few beautiful things left on this earth that make it worth living in. One of the small alluring details that remind me why I should keep existing in a world full of hatred and betrayal in hope that I will at some point discover more of these enchanting things.

Sometimes I feel as though I can only truly confide in the water. I whisper my secrets to the waves as they collide against the rocks, and somewhere in my heart, I know they're listening. Carrying my unheard thoughts down to an undiscovered corner of the planet, a grim pit of millions of years of silently expressed emotion. Never to be found, but never to be forgotten. I guess that's how it's always been.

My mother adored the beach. She'd set me down on the sand as its rough grains scratched my sensitive legs and the rays of sunlight heated my exposed skin, surely giving me sunburns. And we'd just sit there together for hours upon hours watching the tide roll in and out of the coast. Holding hands, and never uttering a word, for the other's company was enough. I think that was the best part, being so close we never had to maintain a conversation.

My most cherished memories are with my mother on that beach. The peacefulness of the faint smell of salt and sunscreen in the air, the sound of all the other children giggling as they nibbled on mint-flavoured ice cream cones and built massive sand castles, only to have them knocked over by the teenagers later that day, and the breathtaking sight of the brightly coloured kites floating through the air in the cool ocean breeze.

But my favourite part was the simplicity of being with my mother all day, admiring the gorgeous oceanfront sunsets, and watching the birds soar through the air, living a life of freedom I can now see I've always craved. A life with no walls being built in front of you as you watch motionless in absolute horror, knowing you can do nothing, because your legs are shackled to the ground with thick steel chains that you realize too late were only crafted by your imagination. Because that's what it's like to be human.

But at the time, my life was just a blur of the pop music blaring from the boombox by the lifeguard's chair, grape popsicles, and SPF 50. It's a life I strive for now, though I know that after all that's happened, I can hardly fathom it. And for that, a part of me will always resent the ocean, although it's still the only place I can find serenity. For that, some part of me will always wince at the mention of water.

Everything has to end eventually. Because, as everyone finds out at some point in their lives, bliss is only temporary. And as I soon discovered, someone's whole world gets shattered into a thousand pieces every day. This time, it was a Tuesday.

I remember the day like I'm looking in a mirror. It's there, all too vivid, staring back at me threateningly as the goosebumps form on my skin. It was the day that changed everything.

We arrived at Eagle Point beach right around lunchtime. It started out much like any other beach day that summer. My mother and I looked for seashells along the coast and named each and every one of them so that we wouldn't hurt the other's feelings. We tossed a gigantic beach ball back and forth for hours. And of course, we sat and surveyed the waves as they crawled up the sand relentlessly, trying to tickle our toes but never quite reaching them, because the ocean always pulled them back into its arms. The start to the day felt deceptively promising.

It was right around 4 o'clock that my mother decided to go surfing. She bought me a grape popsicle and rented a surfboard from the little shop at the edge of the shoreline and scampered into the water.

I remember thinking she was so brave to go surfing as I watched her in awe. I remember the ominous clouds gathering overhead. And I remember my mother being tugged under the surface of the water, drifting away from me, terror flashing in her eyes. I remember the piercing sound of my scream reverberating around the expanse of the beach as I stood there watching my mother as she drowned. I remember the fleeting moment when I decided to save her and hurtled toward her in despair. I remember the strong hands pulling me back from the ocean where my mother soon disappeared. And I remember the feeling of my innocence disintegrating right before me. Everything that happened that day is etched in my memory.

Her death hit me like the tidal wave that took her life. The wave that ripped the surfboard that was my happiness out from under her feet and buried it somewhere in the sand where it would never be recovered.

And ever since then, nothing has been the same."

When I finish my story, I sit on the beach for a while. I stare at the reflections of the twinkling stars on the water I've always found so beautiful as the sea breeze tousles my hair. I'd been burdened with my feelings for too long, and needed to get them out of me. So I came to where it all started, and told my best friend – the ocean.

Part of me feels like maybe my mother is listening too. Absorbing my most profound thoughts like a sponge at the bottom of the ocean where she still lies after all these years. At least, I think to myself, she's where she was always most happy. Floating among the fish in the sea she loved more than anywhere else in the universe. Finally hearing the thoughts I'd had to keep to myself for years.

Now that everything I've been keeping inside of me for years is out of me, I feel empty. But not in a bad way. Because I knew the moment that I started talking something would change. And now, I feel like I'm ready to enter a new chapter of my life, as my mother surely would have wanted.

6 Months Later

Looking back at that time of my life, I shiver as though a chilling breeze is coursing through me, as though I left my jacket with my childhood. And I always try to tell myself that it could have been anyone, that it wasn't my fault. That I couldn't be blamed for what happened that day. Because it's true, it happens all the time. But somewhere at the back of my mind, I still hold myself accountable, because even though the water that day was as clear as the ghost of my mother, I was paralyzed with fear, and couldn't save her.

Still, I've been trying to push through the pain. To convince myself that my mother will always be at my side in memory. Because for all these years, I've been trying to leave her behind, and walk through the door that leads to the rest of my life alone. But maybe life isn't about trying desperately to glue your heart back together. Maybe it's about filling the empty holes that others carved out with new memories. Maybe it's about leaving things behind to make room for better things. And that's what I plan to do.

Since the moment she died, the memory of my mother has been ruling my life like the moon controls the ocean's tide. But still, like the moon, her presence in my heart is what lights up my universe in my darkest nights. Maybe that's why after trying for years upon years, I've never been able to truly leave her behind. Because even though she influences my every decision, she is an essential part of me, like the blood that runs through my veins. And bleeding in the ocean draws attention from sharks. I think trying to forget her has been doing the same thing.

Though thoughts of my mother's death still pollute my mind, I've been trying to step forward and move on. Because tomorrow is a new day, and I'm prepared to walk into it with my head held high, and look ahead to the good things coming in future, instead of looking back at the bad things in my past. I'm ready to take a leap of faith and discover what lies ahead for me. Because I've spent enough time contemplating what's already happened. It's time for me to move forward.

And I'm bringing my mother with me.

Surviving an Earthquake

Sidney Van Dyk

I woke up to the aroma of breakfast cooking. I rolled over and grinned into my pillow. It was only the second day of vacation, and I already dreaded the day we had to leave. The Cuban sun was warm as it shone into my room, and I really didn't want to get up. But I was starved, and whatever breakfast was, it smelled really good. So I forced myself out of bed, got dressed, and headed downstairs to eat. Mom sat at the counter and sipped a cup of coffee while she made faces. "The coffee here is really strong!" she told me, her eyes crinkling with laughter.

The woman who owned our Bed & Breakfast was busy at the other counter as she whipped up what seemed to be a large breakfast. She gave me a huge smile, and waved her hand at me. "Sit, sit!" she said, in a very heavy accent.

I sat, and she set a plate in front of me. It seemed to an omelette. I wasn't sure what was in it. There was something that looked like ham, little black spices (or I thought they were anyway), and vegetables that resembled peppers. The lady, Inez, nodded at me encouragingly. "Eat! Eat!" she cried. I took a hesitant bite. The flavour exploded in my mouth. It was a little spicy, but very cheesy, with little bits of pork and vegetables in it. It was absolutely delicious. She grinned. "You like?"

I swallowed my bite. "It's great!"

As I savoured my omelette, Inez set a cup of pink juice in front of me. I sipped it; it was a little sour. I recognized it as grapefruit juice, and I took another sip.

Mom leaned back into her chair and took a bite of a muffin. "I thought we could just go to the beach today," she said. "Yesterday was so busy, unpacking and everything, so I'd just like to relax. Sound like a plan?"

I gave her the thumbs up, my mouth full of the remains of the omelette.

Just as Mom finished her coffee, the building gave a shake, and the black liquid spilled over the side of her mug, all over the counter and the floor. "Oh no, I'm sorry!" Mom cried as she put the mug on the counter.

Inez rushed over with a cloth to clean it up. "No worry," she told Mom, as she wiped up the spill. But the house shook again, and Inez clutched the counter to steady herself.

Mom looked worried. "Is there something going on?"

Inez straightened and wrung out the cloth in the sink. But it started shaking again, and it didn't stop.

I glanced around. Dishes rattled in their cupboard as the vibration intensified. Inez's wrinkled face looked scared. "Shake!" she yelled. "Shake!"

Mom jumped back as our breakfast plates slid off the counter and onto the floor, where they shattered and spilled food everywhere. I scrambled forward, but the quaking knocked me to the floor. "Sadie!" Mom cried, as I got to my hands and knees. Inez and my mom both held onto the counter to keep themselves up.

The shaking beneath my feet had gotten worse. The house lurched violently, and the cupboards opened, and all the dishes crashed onto the floor, showering us with broken bits of ceramic plates and bowls. I instinctively covered my head with my arms, and fell again, except there were shards underneath me. I felt a fragment of ceramic dig into my skin, and I scrambled to sit up, holding my arm and wincing as I touched the cut.

Mom and Inez were on their knees, Mom with a cut on her cheek. I steadied myself against the wall as my heart raced. We're never going to get out of here, I thought, panicked. The entire house is going to collapse on us! What if – I glanced up as Mom screamed, "Sadie! Look out!" I ducked out of the way as a piece of rotted wood crashed onto the floor next to me.

Dust filled the room as more chunks of wood followed. Inez tried to stand up, but as the house rocked again, she stumbled, her ankle twisting. The crack that followed was discernible over the din of the earthquake. Inez cried out, her eyes glazed over with pain, and she fell into the corner of the kitchen, her head bent underneath her arms.

Mom ducked as decorations fell from shelves. Her face was worried and scared as she looked for somewhere safe. Her eyes landed on a large wooden table in the dining room. She crawled for it, and stopped, and looked back at me. "Sadie!" she yelled, and I huddled against the wall as an explosion rocked the house. "You have to come here!" she screamed. "It's safe underneath! You have to!"

I shook my head. I can't, I found myself thinking. I'll never make it…I'll be hit with something; the ceiling will fall in, and-and-and…

Mom held her hand out to me. "Come on, Sadie! We have to! It will be safer!"

A large chunk of the ceiling crashed to the floor a few feet away from me, sending up dust and small bits of plaster. I glanced up. Every instinct told me to curl up in a ball in a corner. But as another portion collapsed, I got unsteadily onto my hands and knees, and struggled over to where Mom was under the table.

But then I saw Inez, huddled in the corner, with her injured ankle, and I knew I had to help her. I slithered across the floor, which was wet from the water that sprayed out of a leaking hose. After crawling a few inches, I slipped, and fell onto my stomach. I got up again, determined to get to Inez. I moved slowly, careful about where I put my hands.

I reached Inez without falling again.

Inez pointed shakily to the table. "Go," she croaked. "Under table."

I shook my head. "Inez, you have to come too! It's not safe!" I tried not to show my fear as I took my hands slowly off the floor, and grabbed Inez's arm. I tugged on it, and finally, Inez got herself onto her hands and knees, although her injured leg dragged behind her. I helped her along, and we were almost at the table, when the kitchen ceiling completely caved in.

In a moment of complete desperation, fear, and panic, I wrapped my arm around Inez's shoulders and lunged for the dining room. I heard Mom's panicked cry, and I scrambled forward. Then Inez and I both ducked as the ceiling fell to the floor. Pieces of plaster showered us, and I raised my arms above my head to protect myself. Inez slithered across the floor, got underneath the table, and slumped on the floor, moaning. Mom's hands gripped my arms and pulled me across. I curled up into her arms, breathing hard.

Mom's tearstained face was relieved. "Sadie," she whispered, "you just saved Inez." I buried my face into Mom's shoulder and sniffled back tears. Something heavy fell and landed onto the table. I jumped, and Mom glanced up worriedly. Inez held her ankle. She looked horrified at the odd angle and the purpled swelling. I held onto Mom tightly as we waited out the earthquake. It seemed like hours. I jumped at every noise, and it seemed like the only thing I heard were the screams, the explosions, and all I could feel was the earth quaking violently beneath me.

Finally, the quaking stopped and Mom let out a relieved sigh. I wasn't crying. In fact, everything just felt numb. I'm in shock, I told myself over and over. We didn't move. Even I knew that there were still aftershocks. The three of us huddled underneath the partly damaged table for what seemed like days. My mouth was dry, and my stomach felt hollow. All I remembered was Mom holding me and the constant drip of water from the hose. I thought that I could've fallen asleep at one point, but everything was fuzzy.

Suddenly, Mom shook my shoulder. "I think we can get up now," she told me. I crawled out from under the table, while Mom helped Inez. I stood, and nearly fell again. My legs felt weak, like rubber. I gripped the edge of the table until I was sure I could stand on my own. Then, with small, careful steps, like someone learning to walk, I made my way to the door, which had been torn off the hinges.

Outside was a disaster. The rubble was everywhere. Bits of roofs, trees, bricks, vehicles, and other wreckage littered the road. Mom moved to stand beside me, as she supported Inez. "It's okay," she whispered, as I stared with disbelief. "We're alive. Everything will be just fine."

The New Land

Sebastian Pitman

Neechewa walked through the forest. He was 4027 moons old and almost the age of becoming a man of the tribe. But first he had to get his first deer kill. Neechewa had his bow and arrow and his spear clutched in his hands, looking for any signs of movement or colour but saw none.

After walking for a while he heard a slight snap. He froze and silently put a arrow in his bow. He looked in the trees and he saw a flash of grey. His eyes widened as the wolf jumped out in front of him and Neechewa let go the arrow. It hit the wolf in the leg. The wolf yelped and fell to the ground.

Neechewa looked at the pain in its eyes, and he couldn't leave the animal here. He knelt by it and spoke in a soft tone. The wolf looked at him with fear, but Neechewa continued to talk softy, and the wolf didn't move as Neechewa gently wrapped the wolf's bleeding leg with leaves. When Neechewa was done, the wolf stood up and looked at him with grateful eyes.

Neechewa smiled back and then continued on his way. When he looked back he saw the wolf was following him. He said to himself: "Looks like I've made a friend. Wolf, I'm going to call you Jogan."

He still needed to kill a deer before he could return. As they walked, Jogan suddenly stopped and sniffed the air, turning towards the bushes. Neechewa trusted him and grabbed an arrow. He slung it into the notch and aimed it where Jogan was staring. Then he released the arrow. It flew into the bush, and Neechewa ran to find it in the chest of a fallen deer. Neechewa bowed his head and prayed that the animal might rest in peace, then he picked it up and started the long walk back to the village.

* * * * *

Timothy White loved the ship. His mother had cried when he left, but this was a good job for a boy his age. He was at his post in the crow's nest looking out over the deep blue ocean, sailing to what the men on the ship called "the new land". Some of the men had been there before or had heard stories. They described it as a wonderful and dangerous place with red-skinned savages and bears and wolves. "Just like in fairy tales," Timothy thought.

128

From down at the deck, the captain hollered: "What do you see, White?"

Timothy grabbed the scope that he was given and looked in all directions."Nothing much, sir just lots of water."

Timothy went back to day dreaming about the new land.

＊ ＊ ＊ ＊ ＊

Neechewa finally made it back to the village's outer wall and waved at the guardians of the entrance. They looked alarmed and waved their spears towards Jogan. As he entered the gateway, the children and adults backed away from the wolf. Neechewa was starting to explain when the chief came out of his longhouse.

"Hello, Neechewa. I see you have made your kill and found a new friend," he said.

Neechewa told him the whole story and when he was done he set the deer down as well as his bow and spear. The chief told him to put on the warrior's paint and prepare for the ceremony. Neechewa went inside the chief's longhouse and put on the red and black paint in streaks across his face and body.

When he was done he went back outside. The chief was waiting with all the others in the village. Neechewa was proud but nervous. This was the moment every boy strived for. This was the moment he would become a man of the tribe. He bowed his head as the chief repeated the sacred chant. When he lifted his head again, the chief said: "This is

129

the new Neechewa. Neechewa the man. His warrior name will be Beast Tamer."

* * * * *

A couple of weeks had gone by. Night was falling on the ship, and Timothy was on the first night watch. He curled up in the crow's nest, staring out over the ocean. Suddenly he saw a dark shape on the horizon. Land! He gasped, climbed down as fast as he could, and ran toward the captain's cabin. The captain woke up the crew and they took their positions.

As they came close to the land they could make out a small village with fires glowing in the dark. They quietly sailed past it towards an inlet further down the coast and anchored there.

* * * * *

In the morning Neechewa heard some of the men of his tribe talking.

"Last night a large boat passed by our village and is in the inlet on the other side of the forest," one said. "There are men with white skin setting up an encampment there now."

Neechewa had heard of these white men before, but he wanted to see for himself. He fetched Jogan, and they set off sneaking through the forest. He saw that the men had gleaming things strapped to their belts. Then they all started to walk in his direction. He held his breath and lowered himself to the ground out of sight. The men walked right by him with long shining things that they swung to cut through the leaves and bushes.

* * * * *

Timothy was told to go on the expedition to explorel-lage they had seen last night. He and nine other men were hacking through the forest in the direction of the village when he saw a flash. The man beside him fell with a cry, and Timothy saw a arrow sticking out of his back. He turned around to see a man with red skin and a bow in his hand drawing back another arrow It was aimed at him. He put his hands up and dropped his sword. The redskin turned and ran.

* * * * *

Neechewa ran into the village out of breath and terrified. He shouted to everyone that the white men were coming to their village. The women and children ran to hide in the shelter of the big rocks while the men gathered their weapons. When the men heard the telltale sounds of the white men crashing threw the forest, they all drew back there bows. As the pale skins, as the chief called them. crashed into the village, they all jumped out and let their arrows fly.

131

The New Land

* * * * *

Timothy had been in the back of the group, and he could just start to see the huts as they made their way to the village. When they were on the edge of the village, all the men grabbed their guns and checked to make sure they were ready to fire. Then they ran out into the village, but when Timothy burst out he saw that there were many redskins with arrows notched in their bows, and then he watched as they all shot their arrows. Many of the white men fell and so did many of the redskins.

* * * * *

Neechewa ran towards the pathway into the woods. He had seen Timothy backing away from the fighting. When he reached the spot where Timothy was hiding, he stopped. He saw a boy even younger than he was, far from his home and looking terrified. They stared at each other.

Timothy raised his musket and fired it into the air, and all the fighting stopped. He looked at the assembled people, native and English alike. He said to them: "My ship-mates, do not fight! We are the invaders here. Our captain is dead. Let us leave in peace. Let us leave these people alone and sail back to England and to our families."

The white men left as quickly as they came. They trooped out into the boat and sailed home.

S. N. A. K.

Holly Ann Lavergne

9:00 PM – Friday – *The Sleepover*

"Where do you want to sleep tonight, Anya?" I ask my cousin, as we play doctor-princess. She jumps up, her eyes wide awake. Bouncing up and down, her arms grab mine, pulling me up the stairs.

"HUH-AW-LUH-EEE!" She loves the alphabet, and lately she likes to pronounce each individual letter. She squeezes my arm in a tight hug, her curly hair framing a delighted smile.

"Okay, okay," I agree. "Let's take off the princess dress and go get our pajamas on!"

"Yay!" Anya cries, raising both her arms. I pull off the sparkling blue ice queen dress that was layered over a pink

T-shirt and leggings. We race up the stairs to the bathroom, our socked feet thumping over the soft carpet.

"I'll show you my lip balm. This is how it works," Anya says, a serious expression on her face. Her hand delicately reaches into the glass bowl to my right to retrieve her pink lip balm. She unscrews the lid, places a hand on the counter to steady herself as she teeters on the edge of the stepstool. Carefully, she applies it to her lips and then looks at me excitedly.

"Mommy showed me how," she explains. I smile as I think about the time she ate lip balm when she was younger, but I don't mention it.

"Good job!" I say, hugging her. "Now that we've brushed our teeth, are we ready for bed?" Anya considers this for a moment. Her hands are clasped over the ruffled nightgown. She gasps and runs from the bathroom, returning a minute later with two socks.

"I couldn't forget my fluffy socks!" she cries, hugging them as though they were lost friends.

9:28 PM – Friday – *Bedtime*
Snuggled in a nest of stuffed animals, Anya and I are safely tucked in the guest room bed. The light is off, with the door open just a crack and the ceiling fan whirring continuously.

"Goodnight Holly Wolly," Anya whispers.

"Night, Anya Wanya Babanya." She giggles for a moment and falls silent. A few minutes later, I hear a soft snore from the bed beside me. I smile, thinking about how lucky I am to have such an amazing cousin. I fall asleep to the quiet whirring of the fan.

1:06 AM – Saturday – *Where am I?*

I wake to a sharp kick in the back. I open my eyes, confused, wanting to see the comfort of my own room. I look to the right in the dark, trying to spot the outline of my window. Then I see the red light of the alarm clock across the room and am reminded of our sleepover. I listen to hear whether Anya is awake, but her snores are steady, and I lie back into the rhythm of sleep.

1:20 – Saturday – *Not again!*

I am suddenly wakened for the second time by another kick, this time in the arm. The room is dark, and the duvet is piled in a heap over us, so I can't tell which way Anya is lying. By the way she kicked me, I assume she's horizontal. I reach over the mound of stuffed animals to find that I'm right. I try to pull her the right way, but she's too heavy. I don't want to wake her, but I don't want to get kicked again either.

"Anya," I whisper, shaking her gently. "Anya, wake up." I whisper her name a few more times and she whimpers. "Just move this way a little." I pull her limp body over, and she kicks me, this time from the side. Ow! I think. She doesn't fully wake, just whimpers for a moment. Now that she's back with her head on the pillow beside me, we both fall effortlessly back into sleep.

4:02 – Saturday – *So tired…*

"Holly. Hollyyy." I hear Anya's voice, singing my name in a whisper. I groan. It cannot be morning already. My eyelids are heavy and my mind feels thick.

"What?" My voice sounds coarse. I feel like sleep. Is sleep a feeling? My mind doesn't want to think. I open my eyes to see her face hovering right above mine.

"I need my teddy bear. His name is Pinky Bear. It's in my bedroom, but I'm scared to go get it."

Ugh! Really? I think. But aloud I whisper, "Sure, I'll be right back. Wait here." I get out of bed, sad to leave the peaceful warmth of the thick duvet. My feet feel cold on the hardwood floor. I tiptop across the hall into Anya's room, cringing at every squeak.

I push open the door and step lightly onto the soft carpet. Searching the room in the shadows, I peer over the dark butterfly bedspread to grab a worn bear, which I think is pink. Then I repeat the same process until I'm back in the guest room.

I sink into the bed, handing the stuffed bear to Anya. She whispers thank you, and I close my eyes.

4:04 – Saturday – *Need Sleep*

"Holly! Holly! I have to go PEE." I open my eyes, again. Anya is shaking my arm, and I glance at the clock – it's only been two minutes since we last got up. I groan.

"Okay, let's go." I help her off the bed, and our feet pad over the flowery carpet, the hardwood floor in the hallway and the really cold tile in the bathroom. So this is why she wanted fluffy socks, I think.

We reach the bathroom. Anya sits, and I perch on the edge of the bathtub. It hurts to keep my eyes open. Why does the light have to be so bright? When she washes her hands, I just stand beside her, watching blue foamy soap emerge from the princess soap dispenser. I wonder why I was needed for this.

"All done," she says. I take her hand, and we walk the cold floor back to bed. Once she's safely tucked in, we say goodnight and curl up in the pile of stuffed animals and the fluffy duvet.

4:25 – Saturday – *WHY?!*

I'm in the stage between awake and asleep – my eyes closed, thoughts slowing, almost gone. Then I hear a soft voice in my ear:

"SUH-NUH-AHH-KUH." My mind whirs to life. What? No! We can't have a S-N-A-K. It's 4:30 in the morning!

"No, Anya. Go back to sleep. We'll have a snack in the morning," I groan. Now, I suddenly realize what it would be like to be a parent.

"I'm hungryy," she whispers.

"It's too early. We'll have breakfast later."

"Okay," she agrees unhappily, and falls silent.

S. N. A. K.

7:12 – Saturday – *Wayyy too early*

"Holly, the sun's awake. Get up." I open my eyes. Anya's right. It's brighter than before. But it's a weekend – and it's 7:12. That's way too early.

My Aunt must've heard Anya because she quietly opens the door and picks up my cousin. As they leave the room, I hear her shouting: "Wait! I forgot my socks. They're in the BED!" I feel to the left with my bare foot and reach the two socks that she kicked off. I'm too tired to care, and I drift back into sleep.

9:20 – Saturday – *Morning at last*

I open my eyes for the last time of the night. My eyes no longer feel heavy, and I'm as rested as I could be. There are thin rectangles of light shining brightly through the window blinds. I look over at the empty spot on the bed next to me and think about the night. It wasn't really that bad. I stretch out my arms and just lie there, staring at the hypnotizing ceiling fan.

Then I hear three quiet, unsure knocks at the door. I don't say anything. The door is pushed open slightly, and a small head peeps around it. Our eyes meet.

"Hi, Anya," I say.

"Hi, Holly," she whispers, tiptoeing into the room. She has a small pink plate in her hands. She comes closer to the bed, revealing four crackers, each with a piece of ripped bologna placed delicately on top.

138

"I wanted to make a snack for both of us to share because I woke you up when it was too early," she apologizes. "So I used BUH-LO-NEE. Because I like it."

"That's okay," I reply, taking the plate and putting it on the bed. "Come on up." I gesture for her to climb up. Anya launches herself onto the bed.

"I love you, Holly," she says, hugging me tightly.

"I love you, too, Anya," I say, hugging her back.

We both take a cracker and munch happily on the dry bologna.

"Bologna and crackers are the perfect snack, don'cha think?" Anya says.

"Yeah," I agree. We grin at each other.

Eclipse

Angela Yu Fan He

Do you ever look up at the sky and wonder how the sun and the moon came to be? Why there's an eclipse that causes the sun and the moon to form one line? Well, here's a legend, as it was told to me from the stars.

Once upon a time, there lived a king. His name was Skylar. He ruled the world and held the greatest powers that ever existed in his hands. He could make the land move and the sea stop according to his orders. At the age of twenty-seven, he was married to the wealthiest woman to ever step foot on his land, Nightin. Not long after, a baby princess was born. They named her Sun. At that time the word sun meant, "to shine upon the world".

At the same time in the poorest part of the world, another girl was born. Not being able to afford the child, her family left her in a forest at the age of two. They loved her a lot, but they could hardly support themselves. She taught herself everything she knew and she came up with her own name, Moon. She even made a friend, a deer named Eclipse. The forest provided her with fruits and water to live. Every morning she danced among the trees and vines. She loved the forest; it was her home. But not long after the forest was bought by King Skylar. When the guards were surveying the forest, they found Moon and arrested her for being a trespasser.

Every night and day for months in the dungeon below the kingdom, Moon would imagine the life of the people above her. People laughing, singing, dancing, and drinking. It sounded like they were having the time of their lives, and Moon wanted to experience that life. One day, Sun came down to help bring food to the prisoners. She met Moon for the first time. Sun saw Moon as a shy and timid girl who needed a friend, so she helped Moon escape. During the days, they would go to the forest and play with Eclipse and at night, Moon would sneak back into her prison cell.

One day, the King found out. He banned Sun from ever going near Moon again, but their friendship was stronger than the King's orders. During the day Sun would go out to the forest alone to look after Eclipse and when everyone was asleep, she would sneak to the dungeon and play with Moon. Soon the guard found out and told the king. Because the guard wanted the king to be proud of him, he exaggerated the situation. The king was so mad he cast a spell on the two girls, a spell that would send them far, far away from each other. He sent them to the sky.

The king still loved his daughter so he made her seen to everyone. Sun would shine in the day, illuminating the world. During the nights, Moon reflected off Sun. Even kilometres away, the Sun still looked after Moon, never letting go of their friendship.

To this day, the bond between Sun and Moon is still tight. So tight, in fact, that twice in every year they meet. The Sun, Moon and Earth connect in a line, and where the line starts stands a deer, Eclipse.

No Ordinary Day

Crystal Lu

If you had the chance to do the impossible, for better or worse, would you do it?

"Lena, can you go get the mail?" says Mum, her voice ringing through the kitchen.

"OK!" I yell in reply. I twist the door knob and push open our mahogany door, revealing the brilliant sunshine. The emerald grass ripples in the early summer breeze. The flowers are blooming, making it seem like a patch of rainbows, the birds chirping little songs with hidden meanings.

I skip down the stone steps carefully, hoping my clumsiness won't get the better of me. I lift open the azure blue lid, reaching my hand into the painted wooden box. My hand searches the inside of the box and eagerly grips onto something.

I look through the mail, mostly bills. Maybe there's a letter from gran, or a postcard from aunt Autumn. I continue to riffle through the remaining bits of mail, and I find that there's something addressed to me after all! I look over the crisp white envelope for a return address, but there's no sign of who the sender is anywhere. How strange.

I return to the house and place the stack of letters onto the granite kitchen counter. I glance at the round antique clock mounted on the wall. Its hands read 8:17 AM.

I almost jump out of my skin. I'm late! I dash up the stairs in less than 10 seconds and fly into my bedroom. I breathlessly stuff the letter into my backpack and start getting dressed.

* * * * *

I barely catch the school bus, though the bus driver is hardly pleased about that. "You should always be five minutes early! Not barely on time!"

I stare out the window like I do every day, hoping for something interesting to happen. But I'm never that lucky. Bus rides are always so dreary: there are always the screaming teenagers, the angry bus drivers and the never ending stench of gasoline.

I suddenly remember my letter and quickly unzip my school bag, seeing it sitting there, still bright and clean. I carefully tear open the envelope, not wanting to rip whatever is inside it, a letter and a small brown paper bag. I naturally pick up the letter first and put the little brown bag aside.

All the letter says is, "Your time has come; use it well." I squint to see if there are any other inscriptions on the letter. Nope, none at all. I sigh and fold the letter back up. I turn to the paper bag and pour out its contents onto my lap. There's a small bright green four leaf clover, a rusty aged stopwatch, a puffy white dandelion and another piece of paper. Great, is this one going to lack information and explanations too?

"For instant luck, hold the clover and say, 'Luck will come to me', " the paper reads. Instant luck? Is there such a thing? I don't see any instructions for the other two objects, so I tuck them back into the paper bag and stuff it into my backpack.

I stare at the clover. Would this really make me lucky? I do have a math quiz today…I guess it won't hurt. I make sure no one's looking, before I whisper, "Luck will come to me."

A prickly sensation overwhelms me. My head starts to spin, until the bus comes to a halt. I place the clover carefully into my jacket pocket and head off the bus.

* * * * *

Today can't have been better, and it's only second period! During math, it felt like I knew all the answers to the quiz; I'm positive I'm going to pass with flying colours.

Now it's Phys Ed, and things are going great! We're playing basketball (which I normally hate), and people are actually passing the ball to me! And, even more surprisingly, I can actually sink a basket!

The bell rings, and we all run inside. As I'm running, the clover flutters out of my pocket and lands on the cold grey tarmac a few paces ahead of me. I chase after it, but a stampede of other kids run it over before I can grab it. I finally grasp it, but it's been ripped to shreds. I pocket it, hoping nothing changes.

* * * * *

Something is seriously wrong. After I got the four leaf clover back…everything changed. Someone tripped me in the lunchroom, resulting in a huge blue bruise on my knee, Mrs. Selby told me I failed Friday's Geography test, and Cameron Rogers 'accidentally' spilled his cherry soda onto my favourite shirt.

Why did this have to happen? Does it have to do with the clover getting trampled? I head into the hall towards my hook. I dig through my backpack for some tissues, until the little brown paper bag catches my eyes. I open it and the instructions have changed from before. This time, it applies to the stopwatch.

"To voyage across time, hold the stopwatch and say, 'Time will bring me_____' (fill in the blank)," it reads. This day just keeps getting more and more unbelievable. I pull out the stopwatch. It's a silver colour with intricate swirls on the cover.

I just hope this works…

"Time will bring me back to second period," I say. The room starts to spin, and I get another peculiar feeling. My head starts to throb, so I shut my eyes. Only when the room stops shaking, I open them.

I glance at the clock. '10:00 AM', it reads.

My heart skips a beat. It really worked. It's nearly the middle of second period. I navigate through the halls, hoping I can sneak into the courtyard without anyone noticing. I pass by the library and find a bejeweled wallet sitting on the floor.

I pick it up. It feels heavy with money. Who in their right mind would leave a wallet full of money in the middle of the school hallway? I examine it, hoping to find some identification, when I hear a voice.

"YOU! Stop right there!"

I freeze. Was I doing something wrong? I see Mr. Linwood, the vice-principal, and Sandra Honeycott tramping across the hallway towards me. Sandra looks like she is sizzling with anger while Mr. Linwood looks very disappointed.

"Lena Robbins? I'm so surprised by this. I thought you knew better," he says.

"W-What do you mean?" I manage to croak.

149

Before he can answer, Sandra steps in. "You know EX-ACTLY what he means. You, Miss Goody two shoes, stole my wallet! I've been looking for it all day!" huffs Sandra.

My eyes widen. No! This can't be happening! "I didn't take your wallet, Sandra! I found it on my way and I was looking for some identification."

"Then why are you dwindling in the hallway?" asks Mr. Linwood. I gulp, I couldn't answer that. Before I can think of a suitable answer, he sighs.

"I thought you were a good student, Miss Robbins. Now hand Miss Honeycott back her wallet. I have to go make a phone call, to your parents," Mr. Linwood says gravely. I hand Sandra her wallet with my shaky arm. She snatches it with her claws and flounces away. Mr. Linwood stalks off in the direction of his office.

I frantically fly back over to my backpack hook and pull out the brown bag. There's one more thing left. I hope it will fix everything. I've made such a catastrophe! I pull out the piece of paper and the last object, the white dandelion.

"For one wish," it reads, " hold the dandelion and say, 'I wish for_____' (fill in the blank). Then, blow off all of the seeds (and no, you can't wish for more wishes)."

I breathlessly cling onto the dandelion. This is my last hope! I close my eyes and think for a second. I could wish for anything, so what should I wish for? I've always wanted a million dollars, or a kitten…

I sigh. Those treasures will have to wait. I know what I have to do.

"I wish I could begin today again, without the three objects," I say clearly. I take a deep breath and blow off the seeds. The seeds swirl up into the air and circle around me.

I suddenly feel faint, so I shut my eyes. It feels like an eternity until I can open them again.

* * * * *

I'm back on the yellow school bus, I realize as I shake myself from what seemed to be a deep sleep.

Was that all a dream? I guess I'll never know...I gaze out the window, staring into the greens of the grass and the blues of the sky.

I suddenly remember the letter. I wished for the objects to go away, but what about the letter? I unzip my bag and find the familiar crisp white envelope. I tear it open and read the note.

'You've done well,' is all it says.

Ashes to Ashes

Suvi Coulson

"Who? What? When? Where? Why?" I ask, quizzing the shop owner of Andy's Antiques. He puts his hands up in surrender.

"No idea, sir. All I know is that a young man brought that in and said it belonged to his great grandparents."

I stare at the captivating artifact. An interesting urn, definitely an antique. Hopefully I can get it for a good price! I mean, me being an archeologist and all. I shake my head in disappointment. I really want this, but money's been tough these days. I breathe. Calm, Everett, calm. Dr. Everett Eaton, to be exact. I sigh. Take it or leave it?

"Sold!" I say, and pass the man some cash. He flips through the money with a satisfied nod, but before he can say anything, I'm gone. I'm out the door and climbing into my tiny, old car. I set the urn down gently on the floor and stare at my new treasure with glee as I pull out of the parking lot and head home. Score! I quickly pull up my car and head inside.

Setting the urn down, I head into my bedroom with a big bowl of chips to celebrate my little find. I jump into bed and begin to read a book about famous landmarks. I end up falling asleep in an awkward position with my book sprawled on top of me.

I wake to a knocking sound. A hollow knocking sound. Coming from my kitchen. I slip further under my covers. This is really creepy…I hear a muffled voice. What in the world? Curiosity takes over, and I get up to investigate. If I die, I die.

Pushing the bedroom door open, I peek out. Nothing to be seen but something to be heard. The sounds have gotten louder. It almost sounds like…people! How strange! They seem to be arguing, too. I creep into the kitchen and to my surprise I see an old man trying to pull an old woman out of the urn. I'm about to turn away, hopeful that I'm not noticed, and when I go back to bed, things will be back to normal. But, my apartment hates me, and the floor creaks, causing them to look at me. The woman gasps, and pulls the old man back into the urn. I hear more arguing and slowly walk over towards the urn.

"Um…Excuse me? You're in my dream so I think I'm supposed to talk to you?"

The man and woman pop out of the urn and brush some

dust off their outdated clothes.

"Right then. I'm George Decall. This is my lovely wife –"

"I am Regina Decall," she says, cutting him off. George bows, and Regina curtsies.

"Well, I am Dr. Everett Eaton."

The old woman's eyes light up.

"My dear! A doctor! Can you help my husband? Ever since we've died he's been acting strange. I think he's been visiting different urns!"

The husband looks taken aback. "Excuse me, woman! You're the one always visiting the other urns and talking about Mr. Hudson!"

Regina gapes. "He's our mail man!"

George turns to face me. "I need a new wife!" He sticks an old finger at her, and she laughs.

"You wouldn't survive a day without me, George!"

They continue to quarrel as I think about the situation. "Well, I'm no marriage counsellor, but you two need help!"

The man looks at me, face tight with anger. "Well, she died after me, so I get to keep the urn!"

I stop for a moment as what they've said begins to sink in. Died? "You're dead?!" I say, stunned.

The man nods. "We're ghosts, sir." George and Regina grab hands. "Died in 1952." They say in unison.

"Ghosts?!"

They nod. "Will that be a problem? After all, you bought our urn." I stare. The urn? Ashes? Their ashes?

"Oh," I manage to squeak.

George pats me on the back. Then he looks around. "Got any food, Mr. Eaton?" Before I can answer, he begins rooting through the fridge.

I pinch myself.

Regina walks over. "This is no dream, Mr. Eaton. We are real."

I just stare. The next thing I know, my head is spinning, and my legs weaken, and suddenly I've collapsed to the ground.

I wake with a groan. My whole body aches. Sitting up slowly, I rub my fingers across a large bump on the back of my head. The sharp pain causes me to wince ,and I realize that this is no dream. Looking around it seems as though I passed out in the middle of my kitchen floor, and Regina and George just helped themselves to food. Wonderful.

George speaks through a mouthful of food. "Morning sunshine! We just helped ourselves to a little bit of this stuff."

I stare at the plate he holds out to me. Butter. They're eating butter.

"It's delicious! You should try some!" Regina shoves a stick of butter in my direction.

"I'm good. I've tried it, don't you worry."

Regina pulls away reluctantly. "Okay, whatever you say, doctor."

George rolls his eyes. "His name's Everett, woman."

She glares at him. "You best not be speaking to me that way, George William Decall."

"Just eat, Regina!" He barks.

I sigh and ask, "What time is it?"

"12:30, dear." Regina says.

"It's 2:00 AM!" George counters.

Regina narrows her eyebrows at him. "I'm positive it's 12:30."

"And I'm positive it's 2:00 AM!"

I sigh as they start yet another argument. I check my watch. Point: Regina. "I hate to say it George but it is in fact 12:30 AM."

Regina smiles deviously. "Told you so, George dear."

George grunts. "I live with a mad woman."

"What?!" she screeches.

I lie on the couch. It will never end, will it? I decide to close my eyes and think. Ghosts. Elderly ghosts. Elderly annoying ghosts who eat butter. And I thought I was weird.

"Excuse me, Mr. and Mrs. Decall, but I think you both need to go back into your urn so I can have a normal life again." They both look at me like I've lost my mind.

"What?" I ask.

"Well, you see doctor, we may not leave until morning. That's how it works for ghosts. Once we're out, we're out until sunrise."

I let out a huge groan. Great. I have to survive three more hours with these lunatics. I dig my face into my comforter. What else could go wrong?

I jump as a loud crash fills the room. I spoke too soon.

I look up at the now shattered urn in dismay.

They stare at me in shock.

"What are you looking at me for?" I ask. "It's your urn! Plus that thing wasn't cheap!"

"My dear. Now what?" Regina looks at George desperately.

"Well we needed a new one, anyway," he says.

Regina punches George in the arm. "I just got that new couch too! The one with the flowers…"

George rolls his eyes. "Women."

"Okay," I say. "If you guys are finished, we should probably find something that can tell us how to fix your urn."

They nod in unison.

"Good man, Eaton."

Suddenly, George's eyes light up. "That's it! I'll conjure up Edgar, and he'll tell us! He knows everything about these kinds of mishaps!"

George waves his hands around in a strange pattern, and suddenly there's a noise, and a man appears, I'm guessing Edgar.

Can everyone see ghosts? I can't help but wonder.

"Oh, my!" The man cries out. "George? Regina? Who's he?" He points a finger at me.

"No time to explain, Edgar. We need your help fixing our urn before sunrise!" George says, frantically.

"Right then." Edgar nods, and examines the urn. "We need the following items…" Edgar begins naming things, and we bolt around my house in a search of them.

We place the urn pieces and all the other needed items down, and George and Regina recite the spell. In seconds, the pieces are flying together and the urn is returning to shape. George, Regina, and I, gather to say goodbye, and I glance away to check the time. When I look back, everything is gone. But more importantly, everyone.

I wait for them every night after that. Wake up late, hoping to hear muffled voices from the kitchen. But nothing. Not even a trace of them. Then, I realize, my adventure was there, and then it was gone. Disappeared like a ghost.